Death at the Jolly Cricketer

Veronica Vale Investigates - book 7

Kitty Kildare

K.E. O'Connor Books

Copyright © 2025 by Kitty Kildare

All rights reserved. No part of this publication may be reproduced, distributed, or transmitted in any form or by any means, including photocopying, recording, or other electronic or mechanical methods, without the prior written permission of the publisher, except as permitted by U.S. copyright law.

For permission requests, contact: kittykildare@kittykildare.com

The story, all names, characters, and incidents portrayed in this production are fictitious. No identification with actual persons (living or deceased), places, buildings, and products is intended or should be inferred.

ISBN: 978-1-915378-91-0

DEATH AT THE JOLLY CRICKETER

Book Cover by Victoria Cooper

Chapter 1

The itching started when I settled on the faded brown sofa in Mrs Ratchet's neat but dated front parlour in her small, terraced house on Brick Lane. I ignored the unpleasant sensation and focused on my questions.

"I understand Mr Ratchet enjoyed a game of bowls." My pencil was poised over my notepad as I composed my latest obituary.

Mrs Ratchet nodded, a small smile crossing her thin, lined face. "He was a member at the local club on Cheapside. He went once a week, twice if I let him. Sometimes I think he went there because the ale was cheap, not because he enjoyed bowling. But he had friends at the club, and it got him out from under my feet. We've arranged his send-off at the bowls club. The club secretary organised it."

"That's decent of him," I said.

"Well, so he should, since my husband took his last breath there." Mrs Ratchet adjusted her flowered apron ties. "I told him to take it easier, but he got bored sitting around reading the newspaper all day. You know what these husbands are like. Once they stop working, they don't know what to do with themselves. Honestly, I was glad he had something to hold his interest. Having a man around the house all the time is unnatural, if you ask me."

"You had a spirited marriage?" I asked.

"Spirited! Well, I suppose we did. There were fireworks at the beginning, but once you've settled with someone, you find your routine. Don't you think, Miss Vale?"

"I suppose so." I used my pencil to scratch the stubborn itch on the back of my calf.

"Would you like another cup of tea?" Mrs Ratchet asked.

"No, thank you. I won't keep you for much longer." I tilted my head as a faint whining came to my ear. "You have animals in the house?"

"Don't mind them," Mrs Ratchet said. "They were my husband's dogs. I'm not sure what I'll do with them. They make such a mess. I told him I wouldn't let them in the house, but he said they got cold in the kennel. This winter has been bitter."

"Dogs, you say?" I glanced down at my hands. There was a small, black insect on one finger. It wasn't unusual to find fleas bursting to life when the fires were lit, and this parlour was stifling, with a hearty blaze roaring in the open hearth.

I pinched the offending flea between my thumb and forefinger and gave it a suitable end.

"Oh, my goodness! I'm so embarrassed." Mrs Ratchet's cheeks flushed when she saw what I'd done. "I do my best to keep everything tidy, but with my husband's death, the funeral to arrange, and everyone dropping by at all hours of the day and night, I've not kept my usual routine."

"It's quite all right," I said. "I volunteer at a local dogs' home, so I'm used to all manner of parasites. Fleas won't deter me. Although I'll have to make sure I have none on me before I go home. I have a dog, too, and he won't appreciate unwanted visitors."

"I don't know what to do about them fleas." Mrs Ratchet's expression grew mournful. "We've never had them before."

"There are powders you can put on the rugs," I said. "Leave it for an hour and then brush it out. You'll want to apply it to your furnishings, too. And the dogs will need treating as well."

"That sounds expensive," Mrs Ratchet said. "I can't afford to keep the dogs. I don't want to get rid of them because my husband was fond of them, but I don't have time for three dogs. It's like having children! And he never got round to giving them manners, so they're always yipping and pawing at me."

"I should include your husband's love of dogs in his obituary," I said.

"Would you? I'd be ever so happy if you mentioned it." Mrs Ratchet's expression brightened. "He enjoyed long walks with them, although I knew it was an excuse to get away from me when I asked him to do a job around the house he wasn't keen on."

"I always enjoy a brisk walk with my Benji."

Mrs Rachet's gaze flickered over me. "Could ... could you take them? You said you know a place that looks after dogs. And you seem like a good sort."

"We're busy at this time of year," I said. "Christmas hasn't long since passed, and people often get puppies and turn out the old dogs. It's a terrible shame. Dogs are a part of the family, and you don't see elderly relatives shut out in the back garden because they've got long in the tooth, do you?"

"No, I suppose not. That is sad. These three dogs are youngsters. And they're not big. Boisterous, that's what my husband said they were. Would you like to meet them?"

I scratched another flea bite. "Very much so. Lead the way."

Mrs Ratchet led me to the back of the house. The second she opened the door to a tiny kitchen, a small, tan furry face poked out, darted towards me, and barked.

"We will have none of that," I said. "Be a good boy and sit."

The dog stared at me, blinked once, and then settled on his haunches. It helped I had a treat concealed in one hand, which he was already sniffing around for.

"You're a natural!" Mrs Ratchet said. "You're what these dogs need. I'd be grateful if you would take them. My husband wasn't wealthy, but he left me provided for, and I'd be happy to donate to your animal home if that would sway your decision."

I inspected the other dogs. All three were of a similar size, slightly larger than your average tomcat. They were fluffy, in various shades of tan and brown. They looked perky and well cared for.

"We can squeeze them in," I said. "But I'll take them home and de-flea them, so they don't infest the other rescued animals."

"You're an angel," Mrs Ratchet said. "And I know you'll write the perfect obituary for my husband."

"We do our best at the London Times," I said. "Let me get a few more details about your husband, and then I'll arrange transportation for the dogs."

"You're not one of these modern ladies who has a car?" Mrs Ratchet asked as she gently shooed the dogs back into the kitchen before we returned to the front parlour.

"I do, but it's in the repair garage."

"My husband took me everywhere in his old motor. Now, what else can I tell you about him?"

Fifteen minutes later, I had the details to write a thoroughly decent obituary for Mr Ratchet. I placed my notebook and pencil in my handbag and stood. "Do you have a telephone? I need to arrange for transport."

"Yes! We had it installed last year. It's in the hallway."

I nodded my thanks and headed out to telephone Ruby. She'd be working, but I was certain she'd find an excuse to pop over and collect us. Ruby adored dogs almost as much as me.

Lady M's competent and highly trained butler answered the telephone.

"Good afternoon," I said. "Veronica Vale. Would Miss Smythe be available? I have a matter of some urgency I need help with."

"Good afternoon, Miss Vale," he said. "Miss Smythe is not here."

"If she's in the stables, I'd appreciate you fetching her."

"No, she's not at work. She's not been here all day."

"Who is that?" A cut-glass female voice sounded in the background.

"Miss Veronica Vale," the butler said. "I was explaining that Miss Smythe is not working."

There was a scuffling sound on the telephone line.

"Veronica! I'm glad you telephoned." It was Lady M herself.

"It's a pleasure to speak to you. Is there something I can help with?" I asked.

"Indeed, there is! Where is Ruby?"

"I thought she was with you," I said.

"The wretched girl hasn't been here for days," Lady M said.

I hesitated. "I've not seen Ruby for at least a week. She has a busy social calendar, and I assumed some new gentleman had caught her eye and distracted her. Has she really not been at work?"

"Do you doubt my word?"

"Not for a second," I said. "How curious."

"Curious is one way to describe it. When you see her, tell her I wish to have words. Good day." Lady M ended the telephone call.

I stared at the receiver before setting it back in its cradle. Where was Ruby? She hadn't mentioned needing time off work, and she'd been in fine spirits the last time we'd spoken, although she had complained of an unsettled stomach. I'd suggested she cut back on the martinis.

Since Ruby's erratic but trusty driving skills were unavailable, the telephone directory yielded the number for a taxi firm, and I arranged for a collection. After saying goodbye to Mrs Ratchet and carefully attaching leads to the dogs' collars, we were soon on our way home.

The dogs were excited to be out of the house and on an adventure, hopping up and peering out of the windows, their little tails wagging.

I left the cabbie a healthy tip, just in case any unwelcome passengers remained in the taxi, and then climbed out, cajoling the dogs as they yipped and bounced, thrilled to be outside.

"Let's give you a walk to burn off that energy." I encouraged the dogs, who were more than happy to oblige. It seemed they hadn't had a proper walk for days. "You must behave in the house. My mother is fragile, and although Benji is a gentleman, he'll put you in your place if you overstep. And my brother's dog, Felix, won't stand for any nonsense, either."

The dogs wagged their tails, zigzagging ahead of me as they sniffed everything and explored.

After twenty minutes, the walk had calmed them, and I returned home, unlocking the front door.

Benji dashed out of my mother's bedroom, happy to see me, but I ushered him back, not wanting him to get fleas.

I took off my shoes, picked up the bundles of fluff, and hurried upstairs to the bathroom. Once the dogs were safely shut inside, I dashed to the kitchen to grab the flea treatment. I always kept some on hand for Benji and the various four-legged residents who stayed here.

I quickly removed my clothes and soaked them in a bucket with the flea treatment. Then, in my slip and stockings, I dashed back upstairs to treat the three little fellows waiting for me. I'd just got them settled in the bath and convinced them it would be a joyful experience when there was a knock on the door.

"Is that you, Veronica?" It was my brother, Matthew.

"Don't come in. We've got an issue with fleas."

"You've got fleas?"

"The dogs I brought home have. I'll be out in a jiffy. Be a dear and stir my clothes in the bucket downstairs so all the blighters get caught. I'd hate to throw that skirt out."

Matthew grumbled something about not being a washerwoman, but he was more than capable. Laundry wasn't a stretch if he set his mind to it.

As I finished treating the second dog, the smallest and fluffiest of the trio decided he'd had enough and made a leap for freedom. I caught him mid-air, getting soaked.

"Five more minutes for you. There'll be no fleas in this house," I said firmly.

He yipped his protest but submitted to the bath after getting more dog treats and a belly rub.

Once the dogs had received a thorough scrubbing, I changed into dry clothes, bundled the dogs in towels, and dried them off.

There was another tap at the door. "Jacob has just arrived. Do you want me to take over?"

"Thank you. They're almost done."

Matthew inched the door open and peered inside. "They're tiny! I've seen bigger street cats."

"They're some sort of Pomeranian cross," I said. "Nice-natured. But don't let them on Mother's bed until they're dry. And double-check for fleas. Use a comb."

Matthew grinned, his appearance its usual charming mess of unbrushed hair and mismatched clothes. At least he wasn't in his pyjamas. "I'll get to work."

I took a moment to smooth my hair, glad I didn't look a complete fright, then dashed barefoot downstairs to meet my sweetheart, Jacob Templeton, who waited at the door.

"Was I expecting you?" I kissed his cheek.

A small smile softened his stern features. "It would appear not. Have you just got out of the bath?"

"Three dogs. Fleas. Bath time treatment. That's the short version. It's nice to see you. Would you like to stay for dinner?" I called Benji from my mother's bedroom and fussed over him.

Jacob's shift in expression made it clear this wasn't a social visit, so I stopped trying to draw him farther into the house and waited to hear what he had to say.

"I've been thinking about your father." He kept his voice pitched low.

I gestured for him to be quiet. "Not here!"

"That's the problem," Jacob continued. "I know you don't want to discuss this, but we must tell the rest of your family what's underway."

"No, we don't. And don't say another word." I grabbed his arm and led him into the kitchen, firmly shutting the door behind us once Benji was inside.

We'd been discussing the thorny matter of my father for weeks, ever since Jacob uncovered the possibility his death had been by someone else's hand. However, Jacob had no definitive proof, just blurry photographs and unreliable witness statements about foul play.

I'd explained to him several times that, until we had solid evidence, there was no point in worrying my mother or Matthew. I'd carry the burden until we knew the truth. I was more than capable.

"I have another lead." Jacob ran a hand through his dark hair.

"If it's another photograph where you can't tell who's who, I don't want to know about it. Tea?"

"No, thank you," he said. "This isn't a photograph. It's a statement from someone who overheard an argument your father had with another man. Threats were made."

I let out a deep sigh and sank into a kitchen chair. "A threat to my father's life?"

Jacob nodded. "I've spoken to the witness, and I trust him."

"Then pursue it," I said. "But until you have proof, not a word to anyone else. If you upset my mother and she ends up in the hospital, you'll never forgive yourself."

Jacob pressed his lips together then nodded. "You all deserve to know the truth. But I'll hold my silence for now."

Benji whined, unhappy with the tension.

Matthew opened the kitchen door, a dog wrapped in a towel, tucked under his arm. "What's going on in here?"

"Nothing," I said. "I'm worried about Ruby. Have you seen her recently?"

"She's your friend," Matthew said. "You're the one who's always out with her."

"I telephoned her workplace. Mrs M said she didn't show for work. Could she be unwell?"

"That's not like Ruby." Matthew's forehead furrowed. "I expect it's a fellow. Has she met someone new who's turned her head?"

"Not to my knowledge," I said. "Although the thought crossed my mind."

Matthew glanced at Jacob. "How's Margate treating you?"

Jacob smiled. "The office is open. And we're hiring, if you're interested. I could use the help. Veronica has me doing double duty. Investigating cases and tracking down suitable premises for a new dogs' home."

Despite Jacob's grumbling, I'd never seen him so content. After being dismissed from the police following his injury, he'd been a broken man. But now, as the head of our private investigation firm in Kent, he thrived. To keep him even busier, I'd also tasked him with finding suitable grounds to expand the dogs' home. It was a cause close to our hearts.

"I wouldn't want to do any investigating." Matthew wrinkled his nose. "But I'd like to work with the dogs."

The dog he held licked the underside of Matthew's chin.

"You want to work?" I failed to hide my shock. Since Matthew's return from the Great War, he barely left the house.

He glanced at me. "Why not? And I like Margate."

"You're not going to Margate!" Edith, our elderly mother, announced, shuffling into the kitchen far faster than her ailments should allow. "You're too ill to go anywhere. And I'm too ill for you to leave me on my own."

"Mother!" I said with a laugh. "You'll outlive us all."

"My heart grows weaker every day." The telephone rang in the hallway, making her jump. "Who's that at this time of night?"

"It's barely dinnertime," I said.

She shuffled off to answer, and within seconds, her trilling laughter and flirtatious tone told me everything I needed to know. A gentleman she'd befriended in Margate, Colonel Basil Griffin, had kept in touch after our return to London, calling at least twice a week.

"Are the dogs dry?" I asked Matthew. "And no fleas?"

"Yes and yes. Are they staying?" He scratched behind the ears of the dog he carried.

"No. I don't want you getting attached," I said. "Besides, we already have two foster pups. And Felix will get jealous."

"My dog is friendly. And we've got plenty of room."

"I'm taking them to the dogs' home," I said. "Fetch the other two, please."

The moment Matthew left the kitchen, I turned to Jacob. "You're driving. And while we're in the car, we'll be able to talk with no further interruption."

Chapter 2

"I've heard enough. Stop!" I gestured for Jacob to pull out of the traffic and let me disembark.

"It's raining! And cold. And we're in the middle of a discussion." Jacob's hands flexed around the steering wheel.

"What we're doing is going around in pointless circles, and I'm tired of it."

We'd successfully found space for the dogs at the shelter. But as soon as we were on our own with no distractions, Jacob returned to his favourite topic of conversation, revealing the possibility my father was murdered.

"I can't abide secrecy," Jacob said. "It feels as if we're doing something wrong. This business concerns your entire family. They have a right to know."

"What would we tell them?" I asked. "We need evidence. Until we have that, I'm not budging."

"I could tell them myself."

I glowered at him. "If you do, I'll never speak to you again."

"You're being ridiculous."

"Tread carefully, Jacob," I said sharply. "This is my family you're tinkering with. I won't let anything bad happen to them."

He glanced at me, his expression softening. "I know how fiercely you protect them. Your mother's ailments are a constant cause of concern, as is Matthew's poor health. They rely on you too much."

"I want them to rely on me," I said. "And I want them to have a comfortable and safe life. Everyone went through hardship during the war, and we deserve peace. That's what I give them."

"If I were in your mother's position, I'd want to know," Jacob said.

"Then you don't know my mother," I replied. "She lives on her nerves. The slightest stress sends her into a tizzy for weeks. Once, she became so frantic with worry that she had to go to a convalescent home for a month. I was concerned we'd never get her back. Matthew and my mother are fragile and must be treated as such."

"They aren't as fragile as you believe," Jacob said. "And Matthew has expressed an interest in working at the dogs' home when it opens in Kent. And when your mother took that telephone call from her new gentleman friend, she seemed as right as rain."

"You see brief flashes of our lives," I said. "You're not there for the daily drudgery."

"I'd like to be if you'd let me," Jacob said. "I want our relationship to conceal nothing. Not from each other, and not from our families."

"You deal with your family, and I'll deal with mine." I sounded curt, but I was annoyed. "Now, let me out of this wretched car."

"We're still two miles from your home!"

"The fresh air will do me good. Either pull over, or I'll hail a policeman and tell him you've abducted me."

"Now you really are being ridiculous," Jacob said with a sigh as he found a spot to park.

I grabbed my handbag and hopped out, letting Benji out of the back of the car as swiftly as possible. I didn't enjoy bickering with Jacob, but he was wrong. It was sensible to wait and avoid hurting my family. If the worst-case scenario was true, they'd be devastated. As would I.

I dreaded to consider what I'd do if my father's death was at a rotter's hand. My pristine control may well leave me. And that couldn't be abided.

"Please take money for a taxi," Jacob called after me.

"I'll walk, but thank you," I replied. Jacob was a good man and doing his best, but I was so used to being independent and having things my own way that I bristled whenever someone suggested I might be wrong.

"I'll telephone as soon as I have news."

"Definitive news only, if you please," I replied.

I closed the door and watched as he drove away. A brisk walk was exactly what I needed. Despite the frigid air, it would be invigorating.

"We'll get Jacob to see sense, won't we, boy?" I said to Benji, who wagged his tail, always full of cheerful optimism. "He must learn to adapt. We'll never figure things out between us if he continues to be stubborn."

Benji whined softly.

"And yes, I may be a trifle stubborn, too. But so far, it's never done me harm. And I am right about this. We protect those we love."

Benji stopped to sniff a pile of fallen leaves, signalling his interest in this one-sided conversation was over.

Despite our brisk pace, I was thoroughly chilled by the time I turned onto my road. A top-of-the-range Rolls Royce parked outside the house had me slowing. The window rolled down as I drew near, revealing Lady M.

"I'm not accustomed to being kept waiting," she said, her tone sharp but elegant.

Lady M, short for Lady Marie Antoinette Montague-Fortense-Denburgh, was the epitome of classic refinement. She still wore furs and pearls, held balls at her grand estate, and associated with so many titled ladies and gentlemen that I was always impressed she remembered their names and titles.

"I'm sorry for keeping you waiting," I said. "If I'd known you were coming, I would have been here."

"A scruffy chap answered the door and told my driver you'd gone to the dogs' home," Lady M said.

"That would be my brother, Matthew," I replied. "We had three rescue dogs to deal with. Would you like to come in?"

"No, I'm not here for a convivial cup of tea and a shortbread biscuit. I'm still worried about Ruby."

"As am I," I said. "I've yet to hear from her."

"She's reliable but can dip into carelessness," Lady M said.

"When did she last come into work?" I briskly rubbed my arms to stay warm.

"Get in, girl," Lady M said impatiently. "I can't have you catching your death standing in the street talking to me. Climb in. The dog, too. There is plenty of room."

I was glad to slide onto the exquisite leather seats in the back of the warm car.

"There are blankets should you need them for your knees," Lady M added.

Benji settled by my feet, instantly warming them, and I threw a blanket over both of us.

"Ruby hasn't been at work for five days," Lady M said. "Thankfully, it has been a quiet week, or she'd be in serious trouble."

"Did she appear unwell the last time she was in?" I asked.

"No, her usual self," Lady M replied, before addressing the driver. "Carry on, Foster."

"Where are we going?"

"To Ruby's flat. She shares some ghastly little place with several girls. We'll see what they know about Ruby's absence."

"Perhaps she's taken to her bed," I said. "I should have been more diligent in checking on her."

"Ruby is a young, healthy woman with a zest for life," Lady M said. "We have no reason to think she's seriously unwell. You don't think she is, do you?"

"Some illnesses come on suddenly," I said. "I've just been so busy with everything else."

Lady M's gaze sharpened. "Such as?"

"My work. My family. And I'm starting a business. We've set up an office in Kent."

"Doing what?"

"Private investigation."

"Gosh. And who is this we?"

"My companion, Jacob Templeton."

"It's good you have someone suitable. Although, knowing your character, you can achieve everything on your own," Lady M said. "Give Foster directions to Ruby's flat, please. I know the general area, but I forgot to collect the details before leaving home."

I steered Foster in the right direction, and thirty minutes later, we stood outside the shabby terraced house Ruby had rooms in. The building was converted into separate flats with additional rooms for lodgers.

"Good gracious! Ruby told me she lived cheaply, but I didn't think it would be like this."

"The area is respectable enough," I said. "Ruby spends her money on new clothes and parties, so there's little left over for rent."

"There's no harm in that," Lady M said. "Although perhaps I should give her a promotion or some sort of wage increase. Get her out of this dreadful place. It's no wonder she's feeling unwell. I suspect there's damp. I should get my man to look into it."

"Ruby enjoys being in the city. The hustle and bustle suit her."

"Yes, she told me her family lives in the countryside," Lady M said. "Some crumbling old pile with no near neighbours. That would be no fun for a young lady of Ruby's character."

"She would agree with you there," I said. "Let's see if she's home."

After a moment of knocking, a tired-eyed girl of around twenty-five opened the main entrance door.

"Good evening. We're here to see Ruby Smythe," Lady M said.

DEATH AT THE JOLLY CRICKETER 19

The young woman's gaze widened as she took in Lady M's jewels and fur. "She's not here."

"Do you know when she'll be home?" I asked.

"You're Veronica, aren't you?" the girl said.

"That's right. We've passed each other in the hallway before."

She nodded. "I'm surprised you don't know. Ruby moved out."

"Without leaving a forwarding address?" I was stunned. If Ruby had moved, she would have told me. This made no sense.

"I don't think so. Why would she?"

"Could we look in her flat?" I asked.

"Sorry, it's been taken. There's always a waiting list for this place."

"Whatever for?" Lady M held a pristine white lace-trimmed handkerchief to her nose.

"It's good enough for most," the girl said. "I can't show you around. The new tenant wouldn't like strangers poking about in her things."

"I assure you, these strangers have the most excellent reputations," Lady M said.

"I'm sorry, I'd get in trouble." The girl said goodbye and closed the door.

"Perhaps Ruby has gone to her family home," Lady M said. "Let's visit. You're in charge of directions again. Off we go."

I directed Foster to the outskirts of London, a journey of forty minutes. During that time, I happily conversed with Lady M about her estate and the new horses she was interested in. Since her husband's death, her passion had been diverted to horses.

We headed along a short driveway. No lights were on in the main house, which was no surprise, since Ruby's parents often travelled to find work. Ruby's brother had a small cottage on the grounds to live as an independent bachelor, so we could ask him where Ruby was.

"I see someone in the woods." Lady M was squinting into the fading light. "A man."

"That must be Ruby's brother, Todd," I said.

Once Foster had stopped the car, Lady M stayed inside with Benji to avoid the rain. I hurried out, calling to Todd.

"What ho! Is that Veronica Vale I spy!" he called back cheerfully. "What the devil are you doing here on such a dreadful evening?"

Ruby's brother was a tall, broad-shouldered man in his early thirties with a mop of messy hair. He carried a pile of logs, which he set down by the front door of his cottage.

"I'm on an unexpected mission," I said. "Ruby's employer, Lady M, was waiting at my home. She'd like to know where Ruby is. So would I."

"Ruby? Given the time, I'd have assumed she was finishing up at work. Is that not the case?" He glanced at the car, his brow furrowing.

"She's not been in all week," I said. "We wondered if she was staying here."

"No! Come inside. You'll get soaked through if you stay out here."

I stepped inside, grateful for the shelter. "According to Lady M, Ruby hasn't been showing up at work for days. And I haven't seen her for two weeks. We've spoken on the telephone, but not caught up in person recently."

"Gosh. What is she playing at? Cup of tea?" Todd strode into his small kitchen, an unwashed frying pan in the sink, and the smell of fried bacon lingering. It was a typical bachelor setup.

"No, thank you. I'm concerned Ruby may not be playing at anything. What if she's in trouble?"

"Trouble! What are you thinking?"

"Well, she can be impetuous…"

"You're thinking it's a chap, aren't you? I heard about that business in Margate." Todd tutted. "She gets foolish when she thinks she's in love. It's the only thing she gets silly over. Well, and fashion. I can't understand it."

"I've known Ruby for almost as long as you," I said. "She can get overexcited, but she's never silly."

He leaned against the worktop. "I don't know what to tell you. It's been at least three weeks since I've seen her. She got angry because I made fun of her sensible shoes."

"Ruby never wears sensible shoes!"

"She was on that occasion. Clouted me about the ear for teasing her. Are you sure you don't want a cup of tea? Or maybe a nip of brandy?"

"I can't leave Lady M for too long," I replied. "If you hear anything about Ruby, or if she shows up, let her know we're worried and she needs to get in touch."

"It'll be nothing." Todd waved a hand dismissively. "She's caught up in some new fancy and forgotten about us boring old things."

"I'm sure you're right." I smiled briefly. "I won't trouble you any longer."

I dashed back to the car, happy to escape the rain, and found Benji curled comfortably on Lady M's feet. She didn't seem the least bit concerned.

"Any news?" Lady M asked as I settled into my seat.

"Ruby's brother hasn't seen her for three weeks, and she's not staying in the main house."

Lady M touched the pearls around her throat, her expression pensive. "Perhaps she has grown tired of working for me."

"She adores working for you."

"She adores the horses!" Lady M replied. "I don't want to replace her, but things fall apart quickly when they're not looked after."

"Ruby will be heartbroken if she loses her position."

"Don't fret. It's safe. But I wanted her to accompany me to the Mad March cricket match."

"Oh! You're attending?"

"My great-nephew, Thaddeus, plays cricket. He convinced me it would be fun. You have a public house linked to the cricket club. Is that correct?"

"Yes. The Jolly Cricketer," I said. "My father thought it would be fun to learn how to play. But he was always so busy, he never got around to learning. It has an interesting interior. Lots of cricket memorabilia, if that's your sort of thing."

"Not for a second. But I shall look forward to it, although Ruby would have made it much more fun," Lady M said.

"I'll be there. If Ruby hasn't shown up by then, I'll keep you company."

"You do that. But most importantly, hurry and find Ruby. She's such a wretched girl, although I adore her. Foster, take Veronica home."

I settled back in the comfortable seat, my mind racing. Ruby had a habit of being late for everything, but a vanishing act verged on the ridiculous.

Chapter 3

It wasn't a surprise to find the main doors leading into the entrance lobby of the London Times open. The news never slept. The London Times published editions during the worst of the Blitz, the snowstorms of 1915, and the general strikes. Uncle Harry always made sure people got their daily dose of news.

I dashed into the office to see the weekend staff toiling away, hailed them with a cheery hello, and headed to Uncle Harry's office. As usual, he was at his desk, a cigarette on the go and a strong cup of tea sitting untouched beside him.

"I'm on my way to the Jolly Cricketer," I said, "but I wanted to drop off the last of the obituaries." I deposited my papers into the tray on his desk.

Uncle Harry barely glanced up from the copy he studied. "I can always rely on you, Veronica. What's going on at the Jolly Cricketer?"

"It's the charity event. Mad March Cricketers. I invited you to attend and reminded you again last month to put it in your diary."

Uncle Harry finally looked up. He bore such a striking resemblance to my late father that it took my breath away. He was the older brother, his features more careworn. His intelligent eyes were always sharp and his tie always skewed.

"That's the event with the toffs running around the pitch to raise funds for…"

"The dogs' home, as you jolly well know! We cover it in the newspaper every year. We're hoping to top last year's total."

"Good for you. At least the weather is decent. You never know what March might bring."

I'd been glad to discover that, apart from a nip in the air this morning, the sun was out, promising a fine day for cricket. "Join us. Time away from your desk will do you good."

"It may well, but it wouldn't do the paper good to have me shirking my responsibilities," he said.

"The London Times will survive without you for a few hours."

"Don't be so sure about that." His gaze narrowed. "Is something wrong?"

"Why do you say that?" Uncle Harry was a shrewd judge of any situation and had a journalist's instincts when there was a secret to winkle out.

"You're not your usual self. Is your mother unwell?"

"According to her, she's never well," I said. "There are no troubles at home."

"I saw Matthew recently."

"Outside the house?"

"No, I stopped by on my way home. He was still in his pyjamas!"

"He often is. It's good you made time for him."

"Whenever I can, I will," Uncle Harry said. "If it's not the family, what's going on?"

I sighed. When Uncle Harry sensed drama, he was relentless in uncovering it. Part of me wanted to share the information about my father. After all, they were brothers. But there was no point. Why raise his concerns when the evidence was still unreliable?

"Are you taking on too much?" Uncle Harry asked when I didn't respond. "Your activities with the police keep you occupied. As does the dogs' home. You'd be welcome to drop a few hours here."

"And allow the men out there to think I'm not capable." I shook my head. "Work is fine."

He set down his editing pencil. A sure sign he was serious. "You're not leaving here until you tell me what has your brow so furrowed."

If I didn't come up with something, I'd find myself in trouble. "I can't track down Ruby. She was supposed to be at the cricket match today to keep Lady M company." It wasn't an outright fib. I was concerned about what my friend was getting up to.

"Ruby has such high spirits. She's always finding some new adventure."

"That's what people keep telling me," I said. "But I'd like to know what adventure she's gallivanted off on without me by her side."

"She'll be back soon to delight you with her stories."

"I do hope so," I said. "Are you sure I can't tempt you to come to the cricket match? Lady M would find your newspaper stories a joy to hear."

"It's not for me. But be sure to cover the story. If we have room, it'll make a fun filler piece."

I kissed his cheek. "You always give me the best assignments. Now, I must dash. I don't want to be late."

We said our goodbyes, and I left the office with Benji. We took a taxi to the Jolly Cricketer. I'd planned to arrive half an hour before the event began to ensure everything was in place. Not that I needed to concern myself. My landlord, Cedric Bustle, was a hard-working, capable chap. He'd hosted a charity cricket match at the Jolly Cricketer for over twenty years, so he knew what he was doing.

The pub sat to the side of the cricket ground in a leafy north London suburb. The building was red brick with tall, narrow windows. Above the door, a sign with gold lettering displayed the pub's name and a jolly-looking cricketer with a round belly holding a pint of ale.

It was unusual for a pub to be attached to a cricket ground. My mother had been beside herself when my father purchased it, telling him it was a waste of money, but he'd fallen in love with the prospect of learning to play and supporting the charity events. After he died, I carried on with the charity tradition.

I didn't play cricket and didn't have a grasp on the rules, but the men who got involved had deep pockets and donated generously to our causes. This year, the profits would go to the dogs' home. I'd insisted upon it.

"Veronica! We're set for a fine day." Cedric greeted me with a wide smile. He was a mature gent with an old-school attitude but had taken readily to a woman as his employer when my father died. He had a kindly way about him but took no nonsense from troublemakers in his pub.

I gave his hand a brief shake, noticing the fine gold wristwatch he sported. "Let's hope the sunshine makes our players extra generous."

"If they're not, you'll convince them to part with more money." He gestured to the bar. "Everything is in place. The breakfasts are prepared. We'll have lunch brought out at noon and afternoon tea at three o'clock. We'll serve alcohol throughout the day, as the committee chairman insisted."

It was the one thing I didn't approve of. These matches got raucous because of the amount of alcohol consumed. However, a drunk rich man often forgot how much he'd donated and would give more, so I couldn't be too disapproving.

I poked my head into the large dining room. It was set up and ready for our players and their guests. "It looks smashing. And we have an extra special guest attending today. Lady M. Her great-nephew is playing this year."

"Lady M! I shall be on my best behaviour." Cedric curtsied and chuckled to himself.

"She has a fondness for animals, so I'm sure she'll be a generous donor."

"I'll make her an extra special cocktail," Cedric said. "Then she'll forget her airs and graces."

"Don't you dare!"

He roared with laughter. "I'll be back in a jiffy. I need to change a barrel."

"I'll monitor things until you return."

I wandered around the dining room, checked in the kitchen, and spent a few minutes looking out at the immaculate cricket ground. We weren't playing a professional match, but it often got competitive, with each side determined to be the winner of the charity trophy.

The main door to the cricket club opened, and Charles Pembroke strode in. He was the volunteer cricket club chairman, fitting in his duties around a hectic career as a solicitor specialising in property conveyancing.

He smiled when he saw me and walked over. "I knew you'd beat me to it. I take it everything is in order?"

"Naturally," I said.

Charles' dark eyes were warm yet sharp, suggesting he missed little. He wore a tailored suit and carried a bag, which no doubt contained his cricket whites and bat. "I've roped in a few new names. Chaps from my office. They're not playing but will be here as my guests. I've made them promise to give generously."

"Well done! Those are exactly the guests we need," I said.

The door opened again, and Lady M walked in, accompanied by her butler and another lady I instantly recognised, Lady Valentine Demure. She walked slowly but upright, aided by a finely crafted black walking cane with a carved silver top.

Charles's eyes widened, and he leaned in closer. "Gosh! We are pulling in the privileged. Guests of yours?"

"One of our players invited them. If you'll excuse me." I hurried over to greet them, and Lady M made the introductions.

"Is Thaddeus not here yet?" Lady M glanced around the pub, her gaze sliding over the walls and decor. "That boy has no concept of time."

"I'm sure he'll be here soon."

"I expected him to meet me," Lady M grumbled. "And still no sign of Ruby."

"No. Anything from your side?"

"Sadly not. She knows about this event, though. Perhaps she'll put in an appearance and finally tell us what she's been up to, the naughty girl."

"Let me take you to your table, and I'll arrange for drinks. We're serving a full English breakfast if you've not eaten."

"That would be marvellous," Lady Valentine chimed in. "My husband prefers me to eat lightly, but since he's out of the country for a month on business, I intend to loosen my corset and enjoy myself."

"We'll have three breakfasts," Lady M declared. "Is there a suitable table for Julien?"

"Of course. This way." I led the butler to a discreet area just off the kitchen then placed their orders. By the time I'd returned, more people had arrived, and there were many rounds of greetings and handshakes going on.

Lady M gestured me over. "I recognise most of this crowd. That's Sir Geoffrey Langton, isn't it?"

I glanced over at the man in his mid-fifties with neatly slicked-back hair. "That's right. He's a keen cricketer. You'll need to watch when he's playing. He gets ruthless. Knocked a man down once with a ball strike."

"I also know the chap with him. Reginald Harcourt? He's not been knighted, but I believe it's on the cards."

"Indeed. Not only does Mr Harcourt play, but he's sponsoring this year's event, and he provided the prizes and trophy."

"Who's the handsome fellow you were talking to when we arrived?" Lady M asked.

"Charles Pembroke. He works in the city and volunteers as the cricket club's chairman. He's wonderfully efficient and helped pull together this year's event."

"It's good people give up their time for a worthy cause," Lady Valentine said. "Dogs, isn't it?"

"Yes, we're supporting the dogs' home in Battersea," I said. "I volunteer there. It's a wonderful place. Have you visited?"

"No, but I am considering getting a companion. Nothing boisterous. I often amble around the estate on my own when my husband is away. Not that I mind him being away, you understand. But it would be pleasant to have company. The kind that doesn't talk back."

"We've recently taken in three small dogs. They've got delightful characters."

"I'm not sure about three dogs!" Lady Valentine said. "That sounds like work."

"Leave the toil to the staff," Lady M said. "You can walk them and groom them if you so desire. And, of course, they can sit with you while you read, sew, or deal with your correspondence. Then pay someone to do the rest. Isn't that how it works, Veronica?"

I suppressed a smile, thinking about everything I did to ensure Benji's life was idyllic. "It can work that way. Would you like me to arrange a meeting with the dogs? They are delightful."

"Yes, I like that idea. I keep thinking about it, but thinking achieves nothing. I'll have my secretary contact you, and we'll put a date in the diary," Lady Valentine said.

"Who is that haughty madam?" Lady M was unabashedly staring at a beautiful, willowy woman with pale skin and long, dark hair set in elaborate waves. She wore more makeup than was respectable for daytime and a daring silk dress, only partially concealed by an extravagant fur coat.

"I know her," Lady Valentine said with an unimpressed sniff. "Eleanor Pembroke. She used to be a Weaver. Don't you remember we attended her parents' wedding?"

"I attend so many, but I vaguely recollect an event with carved ice swans."

"That was it," Lady Valentine said. "The swans melted."

"With the surname Weaver, Eleanor's ancestors must have been in trade," Lady M said. "Still, there are plenty who make their fortunes in industry."

"Despite being married to your cricket chairman, Eleanor is a dashing socialite," Lady Valentine said. "And if the rumours are to be believed, she's more than one man's mistress. Do you see the diamonds? A gift from an admirer, no doubt."

Lady M and her friend stared at Eleanor as she settled into a seat. An older woman, plainly dressed, accompanied her, her hair scraped back into a neat bun. It was a stark contrast to Eleanor's glamour.

"I've never met Charles's wife," I said. "This is the first time she's attended our charity event."

"Perhaps she's not here for him," Lady M said, a gleam of intrigue in her eyes.

"Someone with so much brass neck would think nothing of supporting her fling over her husband. It's a scandal." Lady Valentine looked around the room. "Which man could be her lover?"

A roar of laughter drew our attention to a group of men gathered at the bar, drinks in hand. Sir Geoffrey Langton was at the centre, regaling the others with a story that had them chuckling and shaking their heads in good-natured disbelief.

My gaze flicked back to Eleanor. Her expression had soured as she watched the group. Which one of those gentlemen had displeased her? And why?

Twenty minutes later, the tables were filled, the air alive with joyful chatter, and the delicious aroma of poached eggs and bacon filled the air as the cricketers and their guests tucked into hearty breakfasts before the match.

Once everyone was happy, I collected a plate of food for myself and joined Lady M at her table after much insistence on her part.

"Ruby is missing a good day," Lady M said.

I mumbled an agreement around a mouthful of toast, but I couldn't shake the feeling not all was well with Ruby. Had she got herself in trouble?

Whatever was going on with her, I hoped it would end well.

Chapter 4

"I was bally well in!" Sir Gerald thumped his cricket bat into the grass. "Anyone with eyes could see I was clearly in."

"I called you out," Reginald Harcourt said. "Be a good sport. You can't win at everything."

"Were you bribed to favour the other side?" Sir Gerald asked. "That's the fourth terrible call you've made. Do you even know the rules of cricket?"

Reginald's expression hardened. "I've been playing since I could walk. I'm insulted you think I'm incompetent or I would take a bribe."

"This is more like it!" Lady M leaned forward in her seat, a glass of champagne in one hand. "I haven't had a clue what's been going on. All these men running around, hitting balls, and shouting. But this, a good old case of fisticuffs, is far more entertaining."

"Quite right," Lady Valentine said. "I like it when men grow masculine and demanding. Unless, of course, it's my own dear husband. Then it's a bother."

After a hearty breakfast, the men headed onto the cricket pitch, forming two teams. They'd named themselves the Trophy Champions and the Kings of the World. Names suggesting large egos were involved.

The game had been convivial, and the teams evenly matched, with the scores reflecting that. It had all been jolly until Sir Gerald grew grumpy after being struck out.

"Are they about to fight?" Lady Valentine stood from her seat, leaning on her cane, excitement in her eyes.

"I won't let it come to that," I said. "I'll send Benji out to stop things."

Benji had been sitting beside me, watching the cricket match, but had slowly fallen asleep. He wasn't a champion of the good old game of cricket.

"If men put half this passion into their marriages, we'd all be happy," Lady Valentine said. "I never understand their obsession with sports."

"It burns off an excess of energy," Lady M said. "The jockeys I hire are the same. So full of vim and vigour that they're impossible to control, but give them a day of training with a fresh horse, and they soon behave."

"Such simple creatures," Lady Valentine said.

"The men or the horses?" I asked.

She chortled. "Both! Although I always favour horses over men."

"As do I," Lady M said. "Much more useful."

They continued watching the dispute on the cricket pitch. I glanced around, unable to settle. I'd been Lady M and Lady Valentine's devoted servant all morning, and as entertaining as they were, they had high demands. I wasn't sure how Ruby managed to be in Lady M's employ full-time.

"Let's carry on!" Sir Gerald called out.

"You were struck out, man! Take it on the chin and sit down," Reginald said. "I won't ask again."

"You can ask all you like, but I'm carrying on." Sir Gerald walked back to his position as batsman.

The other players looked at each other, uncertain of what to do next.

"Be sensible," one of them called out. "It's only a game."

"And it's for charity," someone else said.

"Exactly! It's for charity. No more of these ridiculous rule bends," Sir Gerald said. "Play on, chaps."

"We will not be playing on," Reginald yelled. "I'm the umpire, and my rule stands. If you don't leave this cricket pitch immediately, I will—"

"What?" Sir Gerald interrupted. "You have no power over me. You won the role of umpire in a toss. You shouldn't take the role if you don't understand the rules."

As the men squared off, the first drops of rain descended on the game, and the teams were soon a gaggle of collecting equipment and dashing for cover. Cricket was a fair-weather sport.

"Oh, what a pity," Lady Valentine said. "I was certain they were about to land some punches."

A familiar figure hurried in behind the cricketers, and I was delighted to see an old journalist friend, Dirk Somerville. He hurried through the door, removing his hat and shaking raindrops off it.

"I didn't know you were attending today's event." I strode over and warmly shook his hand.

Dirk was five years my senior, with dark hair already going grey, friendly blue eyes, and a round face. "I've been looking out for you. I hoped to see you."

"What brings you here?" I asked.

"I was hoping to sell a story about the match to a few local newspapers," Dirk said. "I've gone freelance since I came back from the war. There aren't many paid positions around. I've got four more events to cover this afternoon. All sports."

"Of course!" Before Dirk served in the Great War, he'd been an avid sports reporter, especially football. "If you need quotes from me or anyone here, just ask. It may be the making of your story."

He smiled good-naturedly. "The fight on the pitch may raise a few eyebrows in the society column. I can't stand all that tittle-tattle, though. The rumours and gossip. It's not for me."

"Sadly, it sells newspapers," I said.

"Are you still writing the obituaries for the London Times?" Dirk asked.

I led Dirk to the bar and ordered us drinks. "I am. That's one thing you can guarantee will always need writing about."

He shook his head as he accepted his half-pint of ale from me. "Thank you. I don't know how you do it every day. I'd find it maudlin."

"I focus on the people's lives, not how they left this earth," I said. "Cheers."

"And to you and your good health." He took a sip of his ale. "This bunch must keep you busy."

"They have their moments, but this is an annual event, so I'm used to it. My landlord is wonderfully capable. I barely have to lift a finger. Just make sure the guests have a good time."

"There are some notable society figures." Dirk was scanning the room. "You must have clout to reel in so many posh types."

"They're not here for me but for the cause we're supporting," I said.

"Veronica! We need your charm and wit!" Lady M waved a hand at me.

"I'd best go. It would be marvellous to catch up properly. And I could always put in a good word for you at the London Times. Uncle Harry often needs reliable freelancers."

Dirk's gaze lit up. "I'd appreciate that. I won't lie. It's tough out there."

"Say no more. It was nice to see you again." After a brief goodbye, I dashed back to join Lady M and Lady Valentine.

"Who was that chap?" Lady M asked the second I rejoined her table.

"Another journalist," I said. "Our paths crossed during the war, and we've stayed in touch. He's remained in journalism, much like me."

"You served during the war?" Lady Valentine accepted another glass of champagne from a diligent server. "How daring of you."

"It wasn't that daring," I said. "And I'm sure you did your bit, too."

"I should say I did. I had an entire estate taken over by the military. They used it as a convalescent hospital. They left it in a wretched mess. But I suppose it was the right thing to do. Although, I believe the place is now haunted."

"Ghosts! There is no such thing," Lady M said.

"I've seen shadowy soldiers wandering around," Lady Valentine said with a sigh. "I don't mind. I've always adored a man in uniform."

"It was good of you to provide a place for our soldiers to recover. My brother was in a convalescent hospital when he returned," I said.

"Our poor men, they went through so much," Lady Valentine said. "My husband, unfortunately, came back hearty and in one piece. Is it almost time for lunch?"

After the men had changed out of their cricket whites and joined us, it was indeed time for the first course and the charity auction. Local businesses had been generous in donating items, from a magnum of champagne to a long weekend at the Ritz.

Sir Gerald and Reginald continued antagonising each other by bidding on the same things. Although I was happy they did, because the auction items went for extortionate amounts of money. The dogs would be delighted.

While Lady M tucked into her pheasant, I slid out of my seat, murmuring my apologies. I needed a break from the gossip and non-stop small talk. I desperately missed Ruby. She was a dab hand in these situations. She loved getting to know people. Of course, social pleasantries had their place, but I'd been pleasant all morning, and I was out of convivial chat.

I found a quiet corner away from the crowd, Benji by my side. I rested my hand on his head while I breathed deeply and pinched the bridge of my nose to get rid of a looming headache.

"Excuse me, where is the toilet?"

I looked up to find Eleanor's companion standing in front of me. Her expression was blank, her hands neatly clasped in front of her as she awaited my answer.

"Go out those double doors and turn right," I said.

She nodded her thanks and strode away.

I headed to the bar and considered getting something alcoholic to take the edge off but settled for a strong coffee. I was sipping it when Eleanor's companion appeared beside me and ordered two drinks.

"We haven't properly met," I said. "Veronica Vale."

She nodded at me. "Finella Weaver."

"You're here with Mrs Pembroke?"

"I'm her sister and her companion."

"I'm pleased you're both here," I said. "This is for a worthy cause. The dogs' home. Are you a friend to the animals?"

She slid me an irritated glance. "I prefer cats."

"We help cats at the dogs' home, too. I know it's a strange thing. It's called the dogs' home, but there are cats being cared for. Rabbits, too. We help all animals in need. We even had an injured goose a few months back."

"You know a lot about this charity."

"I'm a volunteer. And this is my pub," I said. "We hold the event every year."

"I'm happy for you. Excuse me." Finella picked up a glass of martini and a glass of lemonade and returned to the table to sit with Eleanor, who still looked sour-faced and unamused. I'd not missed that she hadn't made a single auction bid.

I sighed softly as I regarded Finella, stiff-backed and looking like she wanted to be anywhere but here. Not everyone was a skilled conversationalist. I considered myself in that party, so I wouldn't judge Finella for being short with me.

"Are you having a good time?" Charles Pembroke was next to break my attempt at quiet.

I forced a smile. "The event is going splendidly. Apart from the incident just before rain ended play."

"Boys will be boys, as they say." Charles chuckled. He raised a hand to get Cedric's attention. "Can I get you something stronger than coffee?"

"No, I'm fine with this," I said.

He placed his drink order then turned to face me. "If you don't mind me saying, you don't seem fine."

I forced my shoulders back. I was clearly not hiding my tiredness as well as I thought. "It's nothing. Just a trying day."

"I know all about that. What with this club and my work, I rarely have a moment to myself. But I always find time for fun. Perhaps you should, too." Charles's gaze flickered over me before he reached out and traced his finger along my forearm and onto my palm. "I know something that may take your mind off your troubles."

I withdrew my hand and took a step back. "I can assure you, sir, I'm not interested in that sort of thing."

His brow furrowed, and he glanced at my left hand. "You're not married."

"That has nothing to do with it."

"If you're a single lady, there's no harm in having fun. Modern girls all do it these days."

Benji growled, his hackles raised.

"I'd advise you not to say anything else foolish," I said. "My dog is an excellent judge of character, and he thinks little of yours."

Charles blinked rapidly. "Steady on. You're not one of these serious, joyless types, are you?"

"I'm serious about many things, and being taken advantage of by a man I considered above that nonsense is one of them. You should be ashamed of yourself."

He blurted out partial words before adjusting his tie and taking a breath. "I'm sorry if I overstepped. I meant nothing by it. I noticed you weren't with anyone, and I made an assumption. It was an error. I won't make it again."

I gently called Benji to my side. "That is a most sensible suggestion. And I would advise you to flirt with your wife rather than me."

Charles nodded as he picked up his drink. "Enjoy the rest of the event. We will speak later and tally the numbers." He hurried back to his table.

I massaged my forehead with the tips of my fingers.

"Is something wrong?" Cedric ambled over. "This posh lot not being too difficult?"

"Not so much. Is pudding ready?"

"We're bringing it out shortly. Would you like your dish here?"

"No, thank you. If you wouldn't mind looking after things, I need to clear my head and get fresh air."

"You're in luck. It's just stopped raining," he said. "Don't worry, I'll save you a plate of Eton Mess."

"Thank you. That would be wonderful."

After everyone had their pudding and was tucking in, I snuck out of the cricket club, intent on walking off my stress. Benji trotted beside me, never happier than when he was on a walk.

DEATH AT THE JOLLY CRICKETER

I strode in a straight line for fifteen minutes, my breath rapid and my arms pumping. Exercise always made me feel better. Then I turned and walked down the next street, doing the same thing.

By the time I was back at the Jolly Cricketer, my mood had brightened, and I could face the rest of the event with a smile, even if it was a trifle forced.

As I entered the cricket club, I heard a thud and a strangled gasp. I quickly shrugged off my coat, hung it up, and hurried along the hallway to see what was amiss.

Cedric staggered out of the cellar, one hand clutched against his chest. His face was drained of colour, and he was shaking.

I grabbed his shoulder and turned him towards me. "Cedric! What on earth is the matter?"

"I don't believe it. It can't be real," he gasped.

"What can't be real?"

He pointed a shaking hand towards the cellar. "There's a body down there!"

Chapter 5

My heart felt as if it had forced itself up from my chest, hammering in my throat as I asked Cedric to repeat himself.

"I almost tripped over the poor fellow," he said. "I went down to the cellar to see if there were more bottles of the expensive brandy. The men are drinking the place dry! There's no decent light down there, but I know my way around with my eyes closed. But my foot ... it hit something. That's when I saw him."

"Who is it?" I asked.

Cedric turned guilty eyes to me. "I didn't stop to look. I saw the body and some blood, and I panicked. I wasn't thinking." He glanced back at the open cellar door and gulped.

"Perhaps they're still alive! Cedric, fetch some light."

"What will you do?"

"Investigate! If the person is alive, we can assist them."

Cedric shook from head to foot, but after a gentle nudge from me, he hurried off to collect a torch.

"Let's see what's happening, Benji."

With my trusty four-legged friend by my side, I descended into the cellar's cool depths. The stone steps were narrow but sturdy, although I kept my fingers firmly braced against the wall to avoid any falls.

Perhaps that's what happened to whoever was down here. The men had been drinking all day. Someone could have gone looking for their favourite tipple and taken a tumble.

I reached the bottom of the steps and paused, giving my eyes time to adjust to the dimness. Other than pale light filtering in through a coal scuttle opening, there were no windows.

"Hello. Who's down here?"

There was no reply.

Benji was alert beside me, his ears and tail up as he sniffed the air. A sharp, fruity tang lingered, most likely from the wine.

I walked forward and spotted a smart pair of shoes. I hurried over. "Benji, stop. There's broken glass on the floor."

Benji instantly obeyed but remained alert, his attention fixed on the man.

I deftly picked my way around the broken glass, which, from the pungent smell, was from a broken bottle of red wine. As I got closer, I recognised the face. It was Sir Gerald Langton! And from the sickening pool of blood around his head, there was no coming back from this accident.

I crouched beside him and checked for a pulse. His body was warm, but there was no sign of life. I made sure not to move him, but it was easy to see he had a significant head wound. There was also a red mark on his jaw.

"I've got candles!" Cedric crashed down the stairs, grimacing when he saw me so close to the body. "How's he doing?"

"He's gone," I said. "It's Gerald Langton."

"Lord above! The player who had a set-to on the cricket green?"

"That's the chap. Please set the candles around to give us light," I said.

"You shouldn't be down here. It's not proper," Cedric muttered, his trembling hands slowly striking matches.

"Some would say I have an affinity for the dead," I murmured, more to myself than Cedric.

As the cellar brightened, I took my time looking around. There was nothing obvious to cause me concern and certainly no killer lurking in a shadowy corner. I crouched and looked under all the shelving units containing bottles of alcohol.

"What do you think happened?" Cedric bravely stood beside me as I straightened.

"If Sir Gerald fell, surely you'd have found him at the bottom of the steps."

"He could have dragged himself over here," Cedric suggested. "That head injury would mean he wasn't in his right mind."

"Getting to this spot would have taken effort." I turned slowly. "There are no drag marks."

"Drag marks! Do you think someone dragged him or he dragged himself?"

"Answer unknown. His head would have been bleeding, so if he rolled, we'd see that. If not rolled, he'd have staggered and dripped blood. There are no drips and no drags."

Cedric scrubbed at his chin. "I never thought about that."

"How did he get into the cellar?" I asked.

"That would be my fault." Cedric looked distraught. "I normally keep the door locked, but I've been so busy rushing in and out, getting drinks orders and changing barrels, that I left it open. I didn't think it would be a problem. Why would anyone come down here?"

"This isn't your fault," I assured him. "These men are sensible sorts. They know better than to creep around in a dark cellar."

"Not when they're on their fourth brandy," Cedric said.

When examining the stairs, I looked for any indication Sir Gerald had been hurt from a fall, but there were no smears of blood on the steps or walls, suggesting he hadn't taken a tumble.

"Did you see anybody lurking around the cellar entrance?" I asked.

"No!" Cedric exclaimed. "And I don't have sight of the door when I'm working behind the bar. Why do you ask?"

"This may not have been an accident," I said. "Sir Gerald has a nasty head wound, and there's no evidence to suggest he fell."

Cedric's eyes widened. "You don't think—"

"Where is everybody? I ordered a brandy ten minutes ago. Where is the barman?" a posh male voice barked, close to the open cellar door.

"Cedric, we must act quickly," I said. "We can't have people coming down here and seeing Sir Gerald. And we need to get the police involved."

"The police! I didn't think ... If something happened to this chap, they'll need to be here," Cedric stammered.

"Discreetly, make a telephone call and give them as much information as you can. I'll make sure no one pokes around here."

Cedric raced away, leaving me with a moment to look around one last time. Once the police were involved, this matter would be out of my hands, and with Jacob no longer a serving policeman, investigating this crime would be tricky. Although even when he had been on duty, he never made it a simple task.

"What's going on down here? And what's the matter with your landlord? He almost knocked me down." Charles appeared on the stairs.

I turned, attempting to block his view. "We have a situation. Go back to the event. I'll join you shortly."

"A situation?" Charles peered over my shoulder. "Who's that?"

I sighed. Everyone would know soon enough. "It's Sir Gerald. My landlord found him down here."

"Fallen asleep drunk, I suppose?" Charles laughed. "The man can't handle his drink. Gerald, you old drunk, get up here. You've more money to spend."

"He may have been drunk, but he's most definitely not asleep," I said. "He's ... been injured."

"Injured? Why aren't you helping him?"

"We're too late for that," I said. "Cedric has called the police. They'll be here soon."

"Let me see." Charles descended the rest of the stairs and strode past me. He pulled up short when he saw the distressing scene. "Good grief! What happened here?"

"Something unpleasant," I said. "You can't stay here. There could be evidence."

"Evidence!" Although Charles's face turned pale, he remained composed. "I see. Let's leave things as they are. We'll go upstairs."

I took one last, brief look around, then hurried out with Charles and Benji. Charles carefully closed the cellar door and stood in front of it, as though he intended to stand guard.

"You're remarkably composed for someone who's seen a body," I said.

Charles drew in a sharp breath. "It's not my first. Before I pursued a career in law, I trained to be a doctor. Those skills were invaluable during the war."

I briefly pressed a hand against his arm. "I was there, too. Although not in a medical capacity."

"It sounds as if we've both had our share of hardship." Acknowledgement flickered in Charles's eyes. "I'm almost immune to it these days. It makes me wonder..."

"Wonder what?" I prompted.

"Whether I didn't leave a piece of me behind when I came home." He waved a hand, dismissing his words. "Still, we're here now, and we're alive. That's a lot more than can be said for Gerald."

"The police will get to the bottom of it," I said. "Would you mind waiting here to make sure everything remains secure? I need to see how Cedric is getting on. He found Sir Gerald and is reeling from the shock."

Charles nodded and stood alert as I dashed away. I almost collided with Cedric.

"They're on their way," he said.

"Who did you speak to?"

"They put me through to Inspector Harold Finchley. He didn't sound happy."

I reflexively grimaced. "Did you mention my name?"

"I did. That was when he got curt with me."

I gritted my teeth. I'd clashed with Inspector Finchley after a guest at a Christmas party was murdered in the alley beside one of my pubs. "I need to make my own telephone call. I'll be back in a jiffy."

Although Jacob no longer had influence within the police, his expertise would be welcome. I telephoned his house and waited several seconds before the call connected.

"Jacob, I know you have plans to go to Kent, but I need your services," I said.

"Veronica! What's going on?" he asked.

"I'm at my charity event at the Jolly Cricketer. Someone found a guest dead in the cellar."

"Murder?"

"It looks that way. Inspector Harold Finchley will soon be on the scene. I know you two don't always see eye to eye, but he may be more willing to cooperate if you're here. He despises me, so I don't want to make things difficult."

"I'll be there as swiftly as I can."

We said our goodbyes, and I placed the telephone back in its cradle.

I was eager to explore every inch of the pub and cricket club. If this was a murder, I wanted to find the weapon.

Whoever had done this, and the more I considered the scene, the more I realised it wasn't an accident, would have had little time or opportunity. Sir Gerald had been alive when I left for my walk but was dead by the time I returned. Someone murdered him within the last half hour.

And that someone was at this event.

I marched along the corridor to the door leading onto the street, checking everywhere. There was nowhere obvious to conceal a weapon.

Benji remained by my side, ever alert, as he sniffed around. He stopped by a cleaning cupboard, and his ears pricked. I tried the handle, but it was stuck. Most likely locked.

"Veronica, what shall we do about the guests?" Cedric appeared at the other end of the corridor, his hands clasped. "People are asking questions. They know something is wrong."

I pressed my lips together. We should wait for the police to arrive, but if I sprang the news on everybody, I could catch the killer unawares. They wouldn't know Sir Gerald's body had been discovered, and if I paid close attention to people's reactions, I might spot something that led me to the culprit.

"Has everyone finished their pudding?" I asked.

He nodded. "We were about to move on to serving brandy and cigars. Although most of the men have already been drinking my brandy."

"Let's break the news now," I said. "Give people time to adjust."

Cedric's eyes widened. "Should you do that? Won't the police object?"

"Most likely, very much." I walked over to Cedric and patted him on the shoulder. "But one of their friends is dead. If you were in their situation, you would want to know, wouldn't you?"

"I suppose so. I ... I can't do it, though. And they won't believe me if I tell them."

"Not to worry. I'll break the bad news."

"Do you need a stiff drink to settle your nerves?"

"Thank you, Cedric. Not just now. But if anyone else needs one, make sure they're on hand."

"That I can do." Cedric followed me into the dining room, where the cricketers and their guests appeared relaxed, their stomachs full, enjoying the event. Not for much longer.

I lifted a glass and tapped it with a knife until I had everybody's attention.

"Is it time for speeches?" someone called out.

"You're not on the team! No girls allowed," another yelled, earning chuckles.

"If I could have a moment of your time," I began, my voice steady. "I'm sorry to say I have bad news."

That stopped the comments and laughter. All eyes turned to me, and the room hushed.

"There's been an incident. Sir Gerald Langton is dead."

Gasps echoed around the room, and people exchanged startled glances. I scanned the crowd, my gaze lingering briefly on Eleanor's table. Her expression remained sour, as it had been earlier, but it didn't shift into surprise or concern. Was that the flicker of a smile?

"What happened to him?" Reginald Harcourt asked.

"I'm uncertain," I said, "but the police have been called. They'll be here shortly."

"Why do the police need to be here?" my reporter friend Dirk asked from where he stood by the bar, listening intently.

"Sir Gerald's injury was significant. Possibly not an accident."

The room erupted into murmurs, and once again, I scrutinised the faces. Frustratingly, nobody stood out as shifty or suspicious, and no one was missing.

Of course, solving a murder was rarely this simple. The killer would hardly spring from their seat and leap out of a window when I caught his eye.

And if he did, I'd send Benji after him to swiftly resolve this injustice.

"It would be useful to know the last time anyone saw Sir Gerald," I said.

"Yes, it would indeed."

A harsh male voice came from behind me. I turned to see Inspector Harold Finchley standing in the doorway, his expression grim. Beside him was Sergeant Rodney Matthers, who offered me a brief smile. I nodded in return.

"I'm glad you're here," I said. "I was letting everyone know the situation."

"Thank you, Miss Vale. As usual, your services aren't required." Inspector Finchley glanced at Benji and frowned. The man had dreadful allergies and got a swollen nose and watery eyes whenever he was around animals. "I'll take things from here. You keep out of my way."

I was about to protest when Jacob charged in, looking flustered but wonderfully handsome. When had

I started thinking like that? I didn't romanticise. Well, perhaps only where Jacob was concerned.

Inspector Finchley heaved a long-suffering sigh. "Of course. Wherever Veronica goes, there you are. Both of you keep your noses out of this business. I'll speak to you when I have a moment."

As Inspector Finchley barked orders and bossed people around, I resisted the urge to rebuke him. Whatever he thought of me, this was my pub, and my landlord had found Sir Gerald's body. He'd have no choice but to involve me in this investigation.

That was not open to negotiation.

Chapter 6

"It's good to see you again, sir," Sergeant Matthers said as he paused from his task of collecting names and addresses to sip his coffee. "It's been too long."

Jacob looked away from Inspector Finchley, who was stamping about, trying to impress the upper classes and doing a terrible job.

"I'm glad to be back in your company," Jacob said. "Although I wish it were under happier circumstances. You were always reliable when we investigated cases together."

"I like to do my best." Sergeant Matthers glanced at Inspector Finchley, who looked around, his gaze unfocused, as if uncertain why he was even there. "Your replacement has taken time to adjust to."

I cleared my throat to draw his attention and gestured him over. "Inspector, perhaps you would like to look at the body?"

"I know how to run things, Miss Vale. Stay out of my way. An investigation requires preparation. Sergeant, have you finished for the day, or is this an official rest?"

Sergeant Matthers spilled his coffee as he set down his cup. "Sorry, sir. I have most of the names. And Veronica has helped with the rest."

"As nosy as ever, Miss Vale," Inspector Finchley snapped.

"Unfortunately for you, Inspector, you once again find yourself in one of my fine establishments. And it would be unprofessional of me not to take an interest in a death in my pub," I said. "And you should let Sergeant Matthers rest. After all, he's the only one doing any actual work."

Inspector Finchley glowered at me. "Why is it that murders always happen in your pubs? It can't do your already dubious reputation any good."

I clasped a hand to my chest. "I have a dubious reputation? How scandalous."

"Every time I turn around, you're in the middle of a murder. Isn't that suspicious?"

"Only to a chap who's following an incorrect line of thought. It's common knowledge that an excess of alcohol causes people to do foolish things."

"You consider murder foolish?"

The man was deliberately attempting to irk me. "I'd never call it a wise course of action."

"And how do you know for certain a murder has even taken place? Have you been undertaking study recently? Learning the ins and outs of a murder investigation? Or are you jumping to the wrong conclusions?"

"I do not need to be trained as an officer of the law to know when a misdeed has occurred. Now, perhaps I can show you—"

"Find a seat and stop meddling in something that is not your concern," Inspector Finchley interrupted. He turned on Jacob. "And the same goes for you. You have experience on this patch, but I'm in charge these days. I know why she brought you in, but this has nothing to do with you, either."

"I'm not here in any official capacity." Jacob's tone was low and tense as he held in his anger at Inspector Finchley's rudeness.

"Then you'll know to do the decent thing and stay out of my way."

"I was never in your way," Jacob said. "And I didn't come here for you."

Inspector Finchley's gaze flicked to me. "I see."

"You very much don't see," I retorted. "And I insist on being kept informed as to the progress of this investigation. This is a well-respected pub in a prime part of London."

"There'll be few around here who consider it a respectable place to drink if what you're speculating is true," Inspector Finchley said. "And keep bothering me, and you'll find yourself at the top of my list of suspects."

"Ridiculous man," I muttered less than quietly.

"That's quite enough nonsense and chest puffing." Lady M strode magnificently towards us, Lady Valentine trailing behind. "You all know how competent and intelligent Veronica is. I will not have her abilities brought into doubt."

Inspector Finchley startled and took a step back. He made a half bow, his gaze remaining low. "Forgive me, your ladyship. I didn't know you frequented this establishment."

"I frequent wherever I please," Lady M said sharply. "And I always support a worthy cause. That is what today is about. Your blustering is getting us nowhere. We all want to know what happened to the gentleman in the cellar. Murder, you say?"

"Quite right," Lady Valentine added. "We should receive that information freely. Everyone will talk about it, so we must have the latest news."

"I am sorry, your ... your ladyships," Inspector Finchley stammered. "I must gather the evidence before I share information. I can't jump to conclusions and make an error."

"You have Veronica's word as to the circumstances of this man's death," Lady M said. "She's not to be doubted."

Inspector Finchley gave me a vicious glare.

"I know of Veronica's expertise from a most reliable source." Lady M tipped me a small wink. "Although a murder ... so very close to where I stand. It's unthinkable. Are we even safe?"

"I assure you, you'll come to no harm. Not now I'm here," Inspector Finchley said. "The police in my department are the best in the business."

"Because you recently took over that excellent department from Jacob," I said. "He provided them with the training and confidence to do a thoroughly excellent job."

Lady M shook her head. "Yes, yes. I'm sure the men are all excellent at what they do."

"And they always tell us if we're in any doubt as to their superior abilities," Lady Valentine said.

Lady M continued, "How does standing around talking help the dead man in the cellar?"

Inspector Finchley did another odd little bow. "My apologies—"

"Accepted. But I need assurances this matter will be swiftly and professionally dealt with."

"I guarantee it will be," Inspector Finchley said.

"I do not accept your guarantee," Lady M replied. "Not unless Veronica works alongside you."

Inspector Finchley visibly shook. "Impossible! She's an untrained amateur!"

"She is a thoroughly experienced private investigator and runs her own business to showcase her talents. I will pay for her services. She will need access to the investigation details."

"I ... I—"

"I am not finished. I will be unable to sleep for worrying about a criminal skulking around," Lady M said. "The killer will have seen me sitting in my seat enjoying my Eton Mess. He could follow me to my estate!"

"To have his devious way with you," Lady Valentine said.

There was a flicker of amusement in Lady M's eyes. "Inspector, do we have an understanding? Veronica is not to be excluded from this matter."

"I won't get in your way," I said to Inspector Finchley, offering a weak slither of an olive branch. "I've been involved in a fair few cases. You should consider me an asset."

"Veronica has a point, sir," Sergeant Matthers said. "She's been ever so helpful in the past."

"She shouldn't have been," Inspector Finchley grumbled, his worried gaze on Lady M. "Very well. Miss Vale may have access to some knowledge about the case. I accept she wasn't too much of a hindrance when involved in a recent investigation at the Swan Tavern."

I held back my surprise. High praise indeed! "I would like to question the suspects with you. I know some of these people better than you."

"That goes above and beyond," Inspector Finchley said. "You may listen to me asking the questions, but you must not pester. If you get in my way, I won't care who pays your wages. No offence, your ladyship, but I have a job to do, and I intend to do it to the best of my ability."

"I'll be the epitome of discretion," I said. "But if you stumble, I shall shore you up."

"I won't need to be shored up," Inspector Finchley snapped. "Sergeant, finish gathering the list of names and addresses. And find out who doesn't have an alibi. We'll start with them."

"If I may be so bold," I said, "perhaps a peek at the body? You must be certain it was a murder. After all, I am an untrained amateur."

Inspector Finchley's cheeks flushed an alarming shade of pink. "My officers know what they're doing. Let's set to work, Sergeant. We need to thin out this group as quickly as possible."

"Start with Eleanor Pembroke." Lady Valentine had leaned forward and lowered her voice. "She has a unique set of charms she beguiles with. But do not be fooled. She's a vicious little creature beneath the sparkles and silk. I've heard rumours her character is less than noble."

I pointed out who Eleanor was, and Inspector Finchley directed Sergeant Matthers to her table.

"Excellent progress. Now, I must take my leave," Lady M said.

Inspector Finchley hesitated. "I do not think for a second you had anything to do with this matter, but we need to speak to everyone."

"Your fine sergeant has already had a word. Fear not, Inspector. I barely left my seat during the meal, which was excellent, by the way. You must ask the cook if he has any leftovers you can enjoy."

"I will confirm neither of us did it," Lady Valentine said with a small laugh. "We dined together and spent the event admiring the men in their cricket uniforms. Veronica also sat with us. She will support our innocence."

I nodded. I had left the table frequently, including when I took Benji for a walk, but I couldn't imagine two ladies less likely to commit murder.

"Very well. You're both free to leave," Inspector Finchley said. "Please don't take offence if an officer contacts you to ask questions. We need to gather a full picture of what happened today."

"How exciting. A handsome chap in uniform coming to question us! The neighbours will be scandalised," Lady Valentine said.

"You may telephone and make a suitable appointment," Lady M said. "I do not want a policeman turning up on my doorstep unannounced. I, for one, do not enjoy being the subject of scandal."

After Lady M and Lady Valentine collected their furs and handbags, we said our goodbyes, and they left the cricket club.

"Keep this dog away from me!" Inspector Finchley was pressed against the bar while Benji sniffed enthusiastically around his groin.

"If you keep food in your trousers, he'll always be interested in you," I said.

"I do not—" Inspector Finchley pulled half a cheese sandwich from his pocket and scowled at it. "I forgot that was there." Instead of giving it to Benji, he grabbed a paper napkin off the bar, wrapped it around the sandwich, and shoved it back into his pocket.

I led Jacob away from the bar so we could talk in private, leaving Benji to entertain Inspector Finchley. "Would you mind taking Benji for another walk? We don't want to upset Inspector Finchley's allergies or his temper more than necessary."

"I'd like to stay with you," Jacob said. "Inspector Finchley will eventually settle and stop snapping at everyone. I'll be able to talk sense into him."

"Or make him dig in his heels even more. I'd hoped your presence would reassure him, but he sees you as a threat to his abilities. I'll catch you up on everything," I said. "But I don't want Benji to be the reason this goes off the rails, and it feels like it's juddering precariously at a dangerous speed."

Jacob glanced at Inspector Finchley when he let out a hearty sneeze. "I'll take Benji. Watch yourself with Inspector Finchley."

"I have my eyes peeled for any troublesome behaviour." I pecked Jacob on the cheek, patted Benji on the head, and then watched them leave. I turned to Inspector Finchley. "Now Benji is no longer troubling your groin or your nose, who shall we start with?"

Inspector Finchley grumbled something about telling him how to do his job, but I smiled sweetly, twisting to face Sergeant Matthers as he returned.

"I'd suggest Mrs Pembroke," Sergeant Matthers said. "She's not chatty and keeps asking to leave. She could be hiding something."

"I agree. We should begin with the ladies," Inspector Finchley said. "They'll be distressed and won't want to stay on the premises."

"Our fragile feminine minds always fail us in stressful situations," I said.

Inspector Finchley shook his head at me. "Do you have a room we can use to conduct the interviews?"

"Several. I'll make sure one is available."

"Sergeant, see how the other men are doing in the cellar. And we want the body moved out of here as soon as possible," Inspector Finchley said.

I arched an eyebrow. "Once they have collected all the evidence."

Inspector Finchley turned away from me with a grunt of annoyance.

Fifteen minutes later, Sir Gerald's body had been taken away, and I was settled in a small room with the others. I hadn't been given a seat at the interview table but was sent to the corner to perch on a hard wooden chair.

It was another of Inspector Finchley's tactics to irk me, but I would not let the truculent man get under my skin.

We were interviewing Eleanor Pembroke, who had insisted on bringing her sister, Finella, for support.

"I hope this isn't too distressing," Inspector Finchley said after making the introductions and taking Eleanor's details. "We'll be speaking to everyone to piece together what happened to Sir Gerald."

"That's quite all right," Eleanor replied, her voice smoky and soft. "Although I have nothing useful to tell you."

"Did you know the man in question?" Inspector Finchley asked.

"I barely knew him or spoke to him. I noticed him once or twice while we dined. He seemed full of character, always joking."

"He enjoyed a drink," Finella added with a disapproving sniff. "I went to collect our drinks from the bar when it was busy, and he was always there. He was demanding brandy. It's no surprise he fell."

"Did you see him confronting anyone during the event?" Inspector Finchley asked.

"There was a minor incident during the cricket match," Eleanor said after a brief pause. "But we all saw that. Gerald was unhappy about being called out by ... Reginald, was it?" She turned to Finella, who nodded.

"That's what they were arguing about?" Inspector Finchley asked.

"It was barely an argument. In truth, I think they were tired and needed a distraction from all the running around," Eleanor said. "They aren't like you, Inspector. You keep in shape. You must need vigorous exercise to perform your duties efficiently."

Inspector Finchley's cheeks flushed scarlet, and he focused on scribbling notes for several seconds until the colour faded.

"Who invited you to this event?" he asked.

"My husband. He's the chairman of the cricket club. Charles."

"I have a question," I said. "Would you say your marriage is happy?"

Eleanor slid me a glance. "Why wouldn't it be?"

"Attending this event didn't thrill you," I said. "I wondered if Charles insisted you attend as part of your wifely duties. I've not seen you at our previous charity events, but Charles is always here."

"They're happy," Finella interjected before Eleanor opened her mouth. "Charles and Eleanor enjoy each other's company. And I should know. I live with them."

"If you please, Miss Vale." Inspector Finchley spoke in a clipped tone. "Observation only."

I murmured an insincere apology and leaned back. Charles had flirted with me. That suggested trouble in marital paradise.

"Ladies, how often did you leave your table during the lunch and auction?" Inspector Finchley asked.

"A few times, but only briefly, to visit the powder room," Eleanor said. "Ladies need to ensure they look their best at all events."

"I visited the bar several times and took some air," Finella said. "The venue is stuffy, and the noise was giving me a headache."

I sympathised since I'd been in the same position.

"How long were you outside?" Inspector Finchley asked.

"I stretched my legs for five minutes."

"Perhaps you could enlighten us as to what happened to Gerald, Inspector?" Eleanor fluttered her long, dark lashes. "We've heard terrible rumours, but we don't know what to believe. I'm certain a man of your intellect has already figured everything out."

Finella pursed her lips in a show of disapproval. "Some people are saying he fell and hit his head. Is that true?"

"We're uncertain. That's why we're asking questions," Inspector Finchley said. "We need to know Sir Gerald's last movements. Did he seem drunk to you?"

"He wasn't as bad as some," Eleanor said. "Please, Inspector. I'd be so grateful."

As Inspector Finchley hummed and hawed, attempting to find the right words, I studied the ladies.

Eleanor and Finella were short in stature, though Finella was sturdy. If Ruby was here, she'd say Eleanor was a racehorse while Finella was a shire horse. Stout, solid, reliable.

Sir Gerald's death had been brutal, so I doubted either woman had the strength to inflict such a punishing head wound. But I knew better than to underestimate the fairer sex.

When Inspector Finchley failed to reveal more information, Eleanor sighed and crossed her legs, revealing a daring flash of skin. "I would like to go home. My sister is right. This place has no air. We didn't know the man who died, so we had no reason to wish him harm if that's what happened to him."

Finella nodded. "Eleanor doesn't mean to be short with you. She gets terrible headaches, and talking makes the pain worse. We spent our time enjoying the cricket and the food. That's what we came for. Neither of us knew the gentleman in question. So, we'd like to leave."

"Thank you, ladies. I appreciate your time." Inspector Finchley waited until Eleanor and Finella left before his furious gaze turned to me. "Miss Vale. This must stop right now!"

Chapter 7

I smoothed my hands over my skirt and settled them in my lap. "I can't imagine what you're referring to. You told me I could sit in on the interviews."

"At no point did I say you could ask questions." Inspector Finchley drummed his fingers on the table.

"You were unaware of a situation I found myself in earlier today. It involved Eleanor's husband, Charles."

"What situation?" Inspector Finchley demanded. "And why didn't you brief me about it before we started this interview? I need all pertinent information."

"I wasn't aware it was appropriate until you questioned the ladies," I said. "Although, at the time, it felt most inappropriate to me."

"What are you prattling on about, woman?"

Sergeant Matthers shuffled in his seat and cleared his throat, aware of my temper when a man was foolish enough to dismiss my insight.

"Is there something you'd like to add to this conversation, Sergeant?" Inspector Finchley asked sharply.

"No, sir! But I know Veronica. She misses nothing. If she has useful information, it would be good for us to hear her out. It could help the investigation."

"Get on with it, then," Inspector Finchley said. "What have you been withholding?"

I gritted my teeth. He could be such an impertinent, stubborn-headed buffoon.

"Just to clarify," I began, "I wasn't withholding this information. Earlier in the event, Charles was inappropriate towards me. He invited me to spend time with him. Of course, I dismissed the suggestion."

"Why is this relevant to Sir Gerald's death?" Inspector Finchley asked.

"If a man forgets his sacred vows of marriage to someone as appealing as Eleanor, what other morals is he happy to forget?"

"That makes no sense to me." Inspector Finchley set down his pencil. "Why would Charles be interested in you? Mrs Pembroke is a fine, upstanding woman, and a stunner. Don't you agree, Sergeant?"

Sergeant Matthers tugged at his collar, fear in his eyes as he looked at me. "I really couldn't say, sir."

"Besides, the Pembroke name is exemplary. Eleanor's sister," Inspector Finchley checked his notes, "Finella. She said the marriage was happy. There's no reason to think otherwise."

"Other than the proof I presented you with." There was an icy spike to my words. "Or is my name not suitably refined to be taken seriously?"

"You snoop! You ask questions when you're told not to. You meddle in business that has nothing to do with you," Inspector Finchley said. "And you're always around when death comes knocking."

"That last statement is an unfortunate truth," I replied. "Although I'm certain you're glad I'm here now."

"Someone interrupting my investigation, thinking they know how to do my job, never gladdens me," Inspector Finchley said. "You will not ask another question during an interview, or this agreement ends now."

"I was being helpful," I said.

"You were breaking our agreement! Sergeant, you heard the terms of Miss Vale's involvement. Support me on this matter."

"I did, sir," Sergeant Matthers stammered.

"Aha. So I have a witness!"

"A witness is only useful if you're planning on taking me to court," I said. "And you have better things to do with your time than that. Perhaps attempting to solve this murder should be at the top of the list?"

Inspector Finchley's shoulders rose and fell several times before he asked, "What about your alibi?"

I chuckled. "You consider me a suspect? Are you that desperate to remove me from your life?"

"I'm sure I'm not the only one," Inspector Finchley muttered. "This is your venue. You arranged this event. You must have invited Sir Gerald to attend. How do you know the deceased gentleman?"

"This is ridiculous," I said. "You're wasting valuable time by questioning me."

"I will question you for as long as I see fit," Inspector Finchley snapped. "Provide me with the information."

"And if I don't?"

"I'll have you charged with ... meddling!"

I crossed my arms over my chest. "I'm almost tempted to remain silent to see exactly how far that charge would stand up. Please don't tell me you're as foolish as you are unpleasantly stubborn. That combination appeals to no one."

"Perhaps you should answer him," Sergeant Matthers said. "Just to clear this matter up." There was a pleading look in his eyes.

After a few seconds of stony silence, I acquiesced. I liked and respected Sergeant Matthers, and I didn't want to see him unduly stressed. Chasing after Inspector Finchley and cleaning up his messes must make his days difficult.

"Very well. I'll allay your fears that I'm a cold-blooded killer. The Jolly Cricketer has hosted an annual charity event for over forty years. It's a tradition. When my father purchased the pub and the cricket ground, it was a condition of the sale that a charity event took place, and it had to involve a cricket match."

"Why did you invite Sir Gerald to the event?" Inspector Finchley asked. "How do you know him?"

"The event has gained notoriety over the decades," I explained. "Cricket is a gentleman's sport, and as word-of-mouth spread, people were eager to get involved. I never explicitly invited Sir Gerald, but most players are men of influence in law or finance. They spread the word among their peers and encourage charitable activity."

Inspector Finchley appeared unconvinced by this answer. "Was there a personal connection between you?"

"We weren't close. We've met at this event several times, but we don't mingle in the same social circles. Although I was aware of his fondness for dogs, so I expected to see him here."

"I saw on a leaflet that you're supporting the dogs' home in Battersea," Sergeant Matthers said with a smile.

"We are! We're fundraising to expand the rehoming area. We're also considering an investment in Kent. A new shelter," I said. "You must visit when you have the time. There are so many exciting plans."

"That's enough small talk," Inspector Finchley said. "At any point during this event, were you alone with Sir Gerald?"

"Never alone," I said. "I noticed him several times. He was a larger-than-life character with a loud laugh. He enjoyed having an adoring crowd around him."

"Were you jealous of that attention?" Inspector Finchley asked.

I tutted. "I was too busy to be jealous."

"Perhaps you tried to get his attention, and he slighted you," Inspector Finchley said. "You're a proud woman. You would have taken that badly."

"And why would that be? Do you think I had a fancy for Sir Gerald?" I barked a sharp laugh.

"Sir!" Sergeant Matthers said. "Veronica is with Jacob."

"Yes, yes. I know all about that tawdry business," Inspector Finchley replied. "But they aren't married, and these modern women get up to all sorts."

"I may be a modern woman, but I'm deadly serious about Jacob."

"You summoned him here to cause me trouble." Inspector Finchley pushed away his notepad. "He has no sway over me. Not anymore."

I wrinkled my nose at this distasteful and utterly pointless conversation. "I invited Jacob here because the relationship between us is frosty, and you respond better when you think a man is in charge."

Inspector Finchley harrumphed. "It's clear who's in charge around here."

"That would be me. And rightly so. Or did you not see the Vale name above the door?"

"Perhaps in here. And I see who wears the trousers in your relationship, but not in this investigation." Inspector Finchley flailed an arm about, lost in his ridiculous fantasy. "You think you can have it all. You invited a wealthy financier to your event to get to know him better, and when he rejected your advances, you got your revenge."

"Sir, I'm not sure you should antagonise Veronica." Sergeant Matthers looked on with bewilderment.

"It's a plausible theory!"

"It's the most outrageous and incorrect theory you could ever toss at me," I shot back.

"You're always there when the body drops!" Inspector Finchley's tone was accusatory.

"I've been there barely a handful of times. You're making something out of nothing. And if you say one more rude thing about my personal affairs, I shall set Benji on you when he returns." Turning to Sergeant Matthers, I added, "Is there nothing we can do for him? Some further education on how to question a suspect? Or a stint behind a desk dealing with paperwork might make Inspector Finchley realise what a privileged position he's in and not make such a hash of things."

"I won't allow you to speak to me like that." Inspector Finchley's eyes narrowed. "What about your landlord?"

My hands balled into fists. "You devious little—"

"Veronica! We need to learn about everyone," Sergeant Matthers blurted out.

"Cedric has an excellent character." My tone dripped with acid. "He's been here for years."

"He knows the men who came to the event?" Inspector Finchley asked. "Could he have formed a friendship with some of them?"

"The men who come here only notice the staff when they do something they disapprove of or they need something from them," I said.

"Maybe Cedric asked for something he shouldn't have," Inspector Finchley said. "He caused an offence. It started a brawl, and things got out of hand."

"Cedric is a friend to all, provided they drink plenty and pay their bill on time," I replied.

"We'll question him next," Inspector Finchley said. "He could have had a set to with the victim and walloped him on the head."

"That is another waste of time! And you're only questioning Cedric to inconvenience me. That's a petty attitude to have, Inspector."

"You'd question him if you were leading this investigation," Inspector Finchley countered. "Not that a woman will ever have a position of power within the police. Investigations such as these require a level head and composure, and you've shown none of that since I arrived."

"Because I'm dealing with an extremely trying character who would test the patience of a saint," I said.

"As am I. Sergeant, bring in the landlord. Let's see what he has to say for himself."

If I protested further, Inspector Finchley would dig in his heels and make it his mission to ensure Cedric looked guilty. It was better to get this charade out of the way, so we could focus on the genuine suspects.

A few moments later, Cedric was perched on a seat, glancing nervously at me from time to time.

"We've not begun the interview yet, have we, Inspector?" I asked as sweetly as I could.

"Not yet."

"Do I have your permission to speak?"

Inspector Finchley waved at me to continue as he scribbled something in his notebook.

"Cedric, there's nothing to concern yourself with," I said. "Inspector Finchley is talking to all of us to ensure he can find out what happened to Sir Gerald."

"Am I in trouble?" Cedric asked, eyes wide.

"Not remotely," I assured him.

"That's for me to decide," Inspector Finchley cut in. "Let's get your details."

Cedric shared his full name, address, which was the pub, and how long he'd worked at the Jolly Cricketer.

"How well did you know Sir Gerald Langton?" Inspector Finchley asked.

"I saw him once or twice a month during the summer," Cedric said. "He's on a team that plays here. They call themselves the Fancy Financiers. They play and then spend the afternoon drinking."

"Describe your relationship to the victim."

"I served him whatever he wanted from the bar," Cedric said.

"Did you consider him a friend? Did you ever ask him for any favours?"

"He was a customer," Cedric replied, glancing at me. "I knew what he liked to drink, but that was it."

"What's your financial situation?" Inspector Finchley asked.

Cedric hesitated. "I have no problems. Miss Vale pays a good wage, and I have my accommodation above the pub. I want for nothing."

"That's an expensive watch you're wearing."

The fact Inspector Finchley had noticed Cedric's watch surprised me. When I'd arrived at the Jolly Cricketer, I'd also seen the fine timepiece. Most men still sported pocket watches, but wristwatches were growing in popularity.

Cedric quickly hid the watch under his sleeve. "It's nothing."

"How can a man serving behind a bar afford such an expensive watch?" Inspector Finchley asked. "Surely, Miss Vale isn't that generous."

I couldn't hold my tongue. "Perhaps it was a gift?"

"Who do you know who could afford a gift like that?" Inspector Finchley asked, his gaze fixed on Cedric.

"No one! And it wasn't a gift," Cedric stammered. "It's nothing. Forget about my watch."

Cedric's discomfort alarmed me, and now the question was raised, I needed to know the truth.

"It's best to tell us everything," I urged Cedric gently. "Inspector Finchley will only think the worst of you if you don't."

"Did Sir Gerald gift you that watch?" Inspector Finchley asked.

"No! I promise you, both of you. I bought this with my own money."

"Go on," I encouraged.

"My ... my late father was a watch repairman." Cedric's voice softened. "When I was a youngster, I'd watch him tinker for hours. Watches have fascinated me ever since. When he died, I wanted something I'd remember him by." He paused before continuing, "I saw this in the window of a local pawnshop, and I couldn't stop thinking about it."

"You stole it?" Inspector Finchley asked.

"Inspector! Cedric would never do such a thing." I bristled at the accusation.

"I didn't steal this," Cedric said. "I told myself if it was still there in three months, I'd buy it. And I came up with a plan to make it happen. Miss Vale tells me you need to plan for success. Wishes and dreaming get you nothing."

"What was your plan? If you've been working somewhere else to earn extra money, I won't be angry. The pub runs smoothly, thanks to you," I said.

"I haven't," Cedric said. "My work here never suffers. But ... I took a loan from the pub."

Inspector Finchley smirked. "You've been stealing from Miss Vale?"

"No! It was a loan. And I'm already paying it back." Cedric cast me a guilty look. "The watch reminded me of my father. He never raised his voice or a hand to me. He always gave me his time and looked after me. Few of my friends could say that."

I was unhappy Cedric had taken from the business. He could have asked me if he needed the money. "How did you do it without me realising what was going on?"

"The pheasants," he muttered.

"Could you repeat that?" Inspector Finchley raised an eyebrow.

"Every week, we have pheasant pie on the menu. And Mr Pembroke wanted pheasant for the main course. I know a man who shoots his own birds and sells them cheap. It's more work for me to pluck them and remove the lead shot, but they're half the price of the birds from our suppliers."

"You took the full cost of the birds from the accounts and kept the savings you made," I said.

Cedric turned to me. "I'm sorry for deceiving you. I don't want you to think I'm a wicked man."

"We will check your story," Inspector Finchley said. "If you're lying, I'll bring the full force of the law down on your head. You'll end up with nothing."

"It's the truth," Cedric insisted. "I had no reason to dislike Sir Gerald. And I was so busy, I didn't even have time for a smoke break, let alone drag a man into the cellar and clobber him."

"Would you like me to have Cedric charged with theft?" Inspector Finchley asked me, sneering openly. "Or are you content to have your employees taking from the till?"

"Leave that matter to me," I said. "Cedric, you're free to go. But we will speak later."

Cedric shot out through the open door before Inspector Finchley could protest.

Cedric's deception irked me more than I was prepared to show in front of Inspector Finchley, but I wouldn't let it distract me from the case.

"Sergeant," I said, turning to him, "we've collected everyone's details and alibis. Who do we have left as suspects?"

"Must I remind you that you're not in charge of this investigation?" Inspector Finchley's tone was biting.

"Someone must lead," I snapped, "since you're more interested in petty theft than catching a killer."

Sergeant Matthers jerked open his notepad. "We can account for most guests. There are a few who were absent from their tables for more than a few minutes. Long enough to commit the crime."

"Give me the names," Inspector Finchley demanded, still shooting daggers at me.

"Charles Pembroke," Sergeant Matthers began. "He's a solicitor in the city and the cricket club chairman."

"It's not him," Inspector Finchley said. "He's a well-respected fellow and a pillar of the community. Who else?"

"Reginald Harcourt," Sergeant Matthers continued. "He also works in the city as a banker."

"Another respectable gentleman. Anyone else?" Inspector Finchley asked.

"Just because someone is respectable and wealthy doesn't make them innocent," I said. "Don't let a starched white collar and an influential surname throw you off the scent."

Inspector Finchley ignored me. "Anyone else, Sergeant?"

"Eleanor and Finella were seen leaving their table at different times," Sergeant Matthers said, "but we've spoken to them."

"This crime was brutal. It wasn't the work of a female. My experience shows ladies prefer more subtle forms of murder. Poison, for instance, is easy to slip into a drink."

I bit my tongue. I'd thought the same but was unhappy to have a similar train of thought as our bumbling inspector.

"Several people reported seeing a journalist asking questions. I caught him as he was about to leave. Dirk Somerville," Sergeant Matthers said.

"I'll vouch for him," I said. "I've known Dirk for years. He works as a freelance reporter. We met during the war."

"Just because you know him doesn't give him a free pass." Inspector Finchley pushed back his chair. "Let's continue with Dirk."

"We should question Charles Pembroke first," I said.

Inspector Finchley stood with an air of self-importance that made me want to shake him. "Just to be clear, your opinion means nothing to me. You're here because I allow it. You aren't important to this investigation."

As tempting as it was to lash out, I forced myself to stay calm. "Inspector, must I remind you, I have Lady M's support? Should I telephone her and give her a progress report? How do you think she'll respond?"

He almost growled at me. "You are an irritating woman."

"Thank you. And you're a stubborn-headed oaf. Now, let's make the best of things and get on with solving this crime, shall we?"

Chapter 8

With the indomitable threat of Lady M hanging over Inspector Finchley's head, we wasted no more time in planning the interviews. Well, I say plan. Inspector Finchley barked orders, and I feigned interest.

We paused for brief refreshments, and I was pleased to see Jacob was back and talking to the remaining guests, with Sergeant Matthers assisting him. It was like old times, and I knew they'd be gathering relevant information to pass on to me.

Most of the guests had already left, although there were a few curious onlookers lingering, most likely hoping to gather gossip to share during a future luncheon with friends.

Sergeant Matthers pocketed his notebook and headed to the exit. Jacob walked over to join me, with Benji trotting beside him, looking pleased with himself for having two walks so close together.

"I've convinced Inspector Finchley to get things underway, although we'll need to watch him," I said.

A smile flickered across Jacob's face. "I suspect you said the same thing about me when I was in charge."

"I was a trifle critical of you in rare moments," I said. "Although you eventually got your man. And the occasional woman."

His smile widened. "Inspector Finchley can be old-fashioned and sometimes slow, but he's got a decent service record. Give him a chance."

"I'll give him a chance if he gives me one," I said. "Fair is fair. How are the suspects looking?"

"Unhappy and eager to depart," Jacob said. "Some are pulling rank and threatening to make complaints if we don't let them go."

"Inspector Finchley wants to avoid ruffling entitled feathers," I said. "But they must know they need to be questioned. Who's complaining the loudest?"

"Charles Pembroke," Jacob replied. "He's even threatened legal action!"

"The man is in conveyancing. What's he threatening us with? Delaying the searches on a house I may purchase?"

Jacob chuckled. "He has friends in high places and influence. Everyone here does, so we need to tread carefully."

I would tread as firmly as I desired. "Where did Sergeant Matthers go?"

"Inspector Finchley sent him to look for Dirk Somerville," Jacob said.

I glanced around the room. "He'll be close by. Dirk knows the procedure when a crime has been committed. He prefers sports journalism, but he's covered all types of stories, including crime and court cases."

"Inspector Finchley seems interested in him," Jacob said.

"Because Dirk is an outsider," I said. "He doesn't fit with the class Inspector Finchley defers to. Inspector Finchley immediately wrote off Charles and Reginald as killers because of their vaulted city positions."

"He's an old-fashioned sort," Jacob said. "Policing has been his lifelong career. He'll still be in the job on the day he turns up his toes."

"Then he'd better hope I'm not the one who writes his obituary."

"Veronica! Finchley does his best."

"I had to threaten him with Lady M to get any cooperation," I said.

"Use all the resources you have. But don't overstep. I know you enjoy breaking accepted boundaries, but things are different now. I'm not here to assist, so you could find yourself in a prison cell if you don't watch yourself."

"Overstepping is what makes my investigations successful. And you always helped when I joined you on a case."

"Not out of choice." Jacob took my hand and gently squeezed it. "I needed to keep you safe. You have no concept of fear. You race after killers, chase dangerous suspects, and pursue leads with ruthless abandon."

"In the name of justice," I said. "It's a worthy cause."

"Not if it risks your life," he said.

"I was never at risk. I always have Benji by my side."

"And usually Ruby. There's still no sign of her?"

"No, and I'm as worried as Lady M. Perhaps I should report her as a missing person."

"I can make discreet enquiries," Jacob said. "How was she the last time you saw her?"

"As bright as a button, apart from an upset stomach," I said. "The odd thing is when I visited her lodgings with Lady M, the girl we spoke to said Ruby had moved out."

"That's good, in a way," Jacob said.

"I hardly think so. She left no forwarding address."

"People have seen her recently. Ruby must have made one of her spur-of-the-moment decisions. Perhaps she got an offer she couldn't refuse."

"She is prone to flights of fancy. I just wish I knew what this flight involved."

"Look lively! Inspector Finchley is stirring to life," Jacob said.

Inspector Finchley finished his tea and left the empty cup on the bar. He'd spotted Sergeant Matthers's return, and they spoke for a good minute before Inspector Finchley scowled and walked away.

I hurried after him. "Is there a problem? We must start interviewing people before they complain about tardy behaviour and poor policing."

"Did you tell him to leave?" Inspector Finchley rounded on me.

"To whom are you referring?"

"Your friend. The journalist. I expect you warned him to scarper."

"I had a brief conversation with Dirk, but that was before this business began," I said. "He's a splendid fellow and certainly no killer. We should talk to Charles Pembroke. He's being the most vocal about leaving. Perhaps that's because he has a guilty conscience and is worried he'll let something slip when we speak to him."

"You won't speak to him. I'll conduct the questioning as per our agreement," Inspector Finchley said.

"Very good. Shall we begin?"

He heaved a sigh that made me think I'd asked him to do the tango clad only in his undergarments. "Sergeant, please bring in Charles Pembroke."

I held back a smile. "Excellent decision, Inspector."

"The dog stays outside." His glare was frosty as he walked past me. "Remember, not a word."

If I thought for a single second Inspector Finchley was making a hash of things, I'd step in and correct course.

A few moments later, I was settled in my corner seat. Benji remained with Jacob, to avoid a bout of sneezing and complaining from Inspector Finchley. Inspector Finchley and Sergeant Matthers sat on one side of the table, while Charles sat on the other.

"This is a waste of my time." Charles's irritation was clear in his tone.

"You understand we need to speak to everybody," Inspector Finchley said.

"You've let most of the guests go home!" Charles said. "Yet I'm singled out to remain here."

"As cricket club chairman, you have a solid insight into the people who play here," Inspector Finchley said. "Your input could be valuable."

I nodded in approval. It was sensible to soften up a suspect by complimenting them.

"I suppose so," Charles said after a second of silence. "But I don't know how helpful I can be to you."

"We'll rattle through our questions, and then you can be on your way," Inspector Finchley said. "Let's start with your relationship with Sir Gerald Langton. How did you know each other?"

"We met some years ago at a party," Charles said. "I don't remember where. We got talking about cricket, and I told him about my chairman role. He said he'd like to get back into playing. He was on the team at Eton and played for his university team at Oxford."

"Could you describe your relationship?" Inspector Finchley asked.

"Well, I considered Gerald a friend. Not someone I'd invite round for cognac and cigars every week, but our paths crossed at the club and the occasional social event. We always found ways to pass the time." He shifted in his seat. "Why? Have you heard something else?"

My attention pricked, and I leaned forward in my seat. I opened my mouth to ask a question, but Inspector Finchley glared at me. I sat back. So far, he was doing a capable job, so I'd allow him to continue.

Silence swirled around the room. Inspector Finchley clearly knew a thing or two about interviewing people. I often found a pregnant pause caused the guilty party to spill the beans.

"I'm aware you've already spoken to Eleanor," Charles said. "Is that what this is about? You've detained me because of her?"

"You haven't been detained," Inspector Finchley said.

"I'm free to leave?"

"I'd advise against it. As you must be aware by now, Sir Gerald's death wasn't an accident. We need to uncover what happened here."

Charles's forehead furrowed. "If I leave, you'll consider me a suspect?"

"It would be deemed unusual behaviour," Inspector Finchley said.

Charles exhaled sharply. "Blast it, man. She has told you, hasn't she?"

"Your wife was helpful when we spoke to her." Inspector Finchley glanced at me, interest gleaming in his eyes.

"Helpful by ensuring her reputation is untarnished while shoving me in the mud. She's leaving me to roll around and drag myself out of a mess of her own making."

"I wouldn't put it quite like that," Inspector Finchley said.

I was almost bouncing in my seat, so desperate to ask a question. I knew there was more to their happy façade of a marriage than met the eye. Not only had Charles openly flirted with me, but I'd noticed he wasn't wearing his wedding ring.

"I won't have my reputation left in tatters because of her lies," Charles said. "Recently, it's got out of hand, and I'm done with it. This murder is the cherry on the cake."

"If your wife is speaking untruths, I'll pay them no attention," Inspector Finchley said. "But you must clarify what you mean, so I may proceed with caution."

"Don't listen to anything she says," Charles spat out. "Thirty years ago, this sort of behaviour would have seen her sent to an asylum. It's humiliating. And it shows an unstable character. She has a complete disregard for everything I've provided her with. My mother told me I was making a mistake by marrying Eleanor."

"Please don't take offence, but a reliable source informed me Eleanor is a socialite. It's given her a reputation not every husband would be proud of." I shot a mildly apologetic look at Inspector Finchley, but this line of questioning needed pursuing.

"That's how we met." Charles glanced over his shoulder at me. "Are you reporting on this murder for a story?"

"No, I'm assisting the police," I said. "I have a private investigation firm, and Lady M requested my services to discover what happened."

"Gosh! A woman detective. Look out, Inspector, she'll be after your job next."

"I'm always on my guard around Miss Vale," Inspector Finchley said dryly. "Now—"

"Sorry for cutting you off, Inspector," I said. "Charles, am I right in thinking you're unhappy because your wife involves herself with other men?"

"It's a disgrace! A humiliation!" Charles said bitterly. "And do you want to know the worst of it?"

"Absolutely!"

"Eleanor has said repeatedly that I'm not man enough for her and she'll find someone more suitable." Charles barked a dry, hard laugh. "She needs to hurry because she's not getting any younger or prettier."

"Was she involved with Sir Gerald?" I asked.

Charles adjusted the cuffs of his smart shirt. "I knew she'd brag about it. She has an eye for the older man, knowing they are more established with their social connections and have deeper pockets. Why? I give her everything she demands. The house in central London, a summer place in Italy I can barely afford, and all the jewels she desires. She always wants more. I told her enough. That was when she cast her net to see who she could catch. Did she say terrible things about me?"

"Your wife said you had a happy marriage," Inspector Finchley said.

"It was Finella who mentioned that," I said.

"Oh! Really? The way you talked, it sounded like she'd made me the guilty party. The jealous husband hellbent on getting revenge."

"Your wife said little to us," Inspector Finchley said. "I appreciate you being so forthcoming, though."

Confusion crossed Charles's face. "Drat! But I don't understand. Why did you question her if you didn't know about their affair?"

"We're speaking to everybody who left their table for more than a few minutes," I said.

"Oh!" Charles's eyes widened. "Do you think Eleanor did it?"

"I consider that to be highly unlikely," Inspector Finchley said. "But we must gather all the information."

"I see. Well, my wife is many things. A gold digger, a harlot, heartless. But she's not a killer," Charles said, looking at Inspector Finchley. "Is she?"

"I don't believe your wife did this. The method used suggests a man's involvement. The blow that killed Sir Gerald was brutal."

Charles grimaced as he slumped in his seat. "I was joking about the jealous husband bit. Poor taste, I know. I suppose she mentioned the fight?"

Inspector Finchley shook his head. "What fight would that be, sir?"

Charles tipped back his head and sighed. "Double drat! I thought she'd want me in trouble. Forget I said anything."

"We'd appreciate your honesty," Inspector Finchley said.

Charles crossed his arms over his chest. "I'm inclined not to tell you. I feel you've tricked me."

"Silence makes a person look guilty," I said.

He flung up his hands. "Very well. It was nothing. We had words about a business deal. I wanted to go in one direction and he wanted to go in the other. We cleared things up. It was all civilised."

"Someone reported that you left the luncheon," I said. "Where did you go?"

"Who said that? Eleanor?"

"Not Eleanor." Inspector Finchley jumped in before I could continue. "Other diners mentioned seeing you slipping out."

"I didn't slip out!" Charles said. "You make me sound like a shifty cad. Sometimes, business waits for no man. I had urgent telephone calls to make."

"Where did you make those telephone calls?" I asked. "We have a telephone available at the bar."

"I tried the line, but somebody else was on it. I had to use the public telephone box down the road. It was most inconvenient."

"Thank you. That's helpful," Inspector Finchley said.

"We can check your use of that telephone." I didn't look at Inspector Finchley for confirmation, hoping the mild threat would encourage Charles not to keep any more secrets.

"Do so. And then remove me from your list of suspects," Charles said. "I had nothing to do with this dreadful business."

"Would you do that?" I asked.

"Whatever do you mean?" Charles asked.

"If you were investigating a murder and learned Inspector Finchley's wife was having an affair with the murdered man, wouldn't you be interested in him for the crime? After all, he'd been humiliated repeatedly. Perhaps he snapped."

Charles blasted out several words that made no sense before muttering, "It wasn't me."

"Thank you for that valuable insight, Miss Vale." Inspector Finchley stood. "Mr Pembroke, if you think of anything else useful, please let us know. We'll be in touch."

Charles looked from me to Inspector Finchley and back again. "I didn't do this."

"Thank you for your time, sir," Inspector Finchley said, opening the door.

After a second's pause, Charles stood and hurried out, buttoning his jacket. Inspector Finchley closed the door and turned to me.

"I know. I didn't keep quiet, but we did excellent work," I said. "The affair between Eleanor and Sir Gerald makes Charles our prime suspect."

"This makes him nothing to you," Inspector Finchley said. "You can leave, too."

Before I voiced my protest, there was a knock on the door, and Jacob stepped in. "Did Charles tell you about the fight?"

"He mentioned a small business disagreement with Sir Gerald," I said.

"This is something significant. I've been speaking to the waiter who served their table. You'll all want to hear this."

Chapter 9

After a quick check on Benji, who was happy to stay with Cedric, providing there was a regular offering of treats, we convened in a private parlour in the Jolly Cricketer.

The waiter Jacob had questioned stood before us, nervously twisting his white gloves in his hands. He was a young man, perhaps twenty, with ruddy cheeks. I doubted he often needed to shave. His well-fitting waistcoat showed he was thin, and he held himself with rigid propriety, expected in establishments like this.

"Let's start by you repeating what you said to Mr Templeton." Inspector Finchley emphasised the word, mister. He was trying to put Jacob in his place. Foolish man.

The waiter swallowed and darted a glance at Jacob, who was seated beside me.

Jacob offered the waiter a reassuring nod. I kept my expression neutral but attentive, trying to encourage the boy without the faintest suggestion of interference.

It worked. The young man straightened his shoulders and began. "It was after the first course, sir. Everyone was enjoying themselves. That was when I noticed Sir Gerald. That's the gentleman who—"

"Yes, yes, we know who Sir Gerald Langton is," Inspector Finchley said. "Get to the point."

The waiter faltered, but Jacob interjected. "Take your time, lad. What did you notice about Sir Gerald? Tell them what you said to me. You won't get in trouble."

"Sir Gerald was with a group of men. Most of them had played in the match earlier in the day. He snuck out through a side door into the garden that runs along the side of the club. I didn't think much of it at first and thought he was stretching his legs between courses. Then I saw Mr Pembroke—"

"Charles Pembroke?" I clarified, leaning forward slightly.

"Yes, Miss Vale. He went after him, but he wasn't looking for fresh air, if you take my meaning. He looked ... furious. Red as a beetroot and striding like he meant to settle a score."

I exchanged a glance with Jacob. This was significant.

"And did he?" Jacob prompted. "Settle a score?"

The waiter hesitated, his hands tightening on his crumpled white serving gloves. "I saw them in the far corner of the garden. I couldn't hear everything they said, but their voices were raised, so I heard some of it. Mr Pembroke accused Sir Gerald of being a scoundrel. He called him a scoundrel and worse."

"How much worse?" Inspector Finchley's pencil scratched against his notepad with an urgency that didn't match his usual lacklustre demeanour when crime solving.

The waiter glanced at the inspector then at me. "I don't like to say in front of a lady. They exchanged cuss words."

I gave him an encouraging smile. "Tell us everything. It's important. It could help us catch a killer."

"Well, Mr Pembroke said something about a slight to his character and an embarrassment. He was shouting at this point. Everyone else was inside, so I don't think they heard, but I was near enough."

"And then?" Inspector Finchley asked.

"Sir Gerald laughed. Right in his face. He said it wasn't his fault and the man was a fool."

"And how did Mr Pembroke respond?" I asked.

"He ... he said he'd teach Sir Gerald a lesson he'd never forget."

Jacob let out a low whistle while Inspector Finchley's expression darkened. I stayed quiet, letting the boy finish. He could have more information.

"That's when Mr Pembroke got even angrier," the waiter continued. "He took a swing at Sir Gerald! Caught him right across the jaw. And when Sir Gerald tried to fight back, Mr Pembroke shoved him so hard he fell and landed flat on his back in the flowerbed."

"There was a mark on Sir Gerald's jaw that would be consistent with a fist strike," I said. "That could have been from this fight."

"You're an injury specialist and a detective? Will your talents never cease?" Inspector Finchley asked, with no small degree of sharpness.

"I amaze myself daily," I retorted. "This shows Charles has a temper. One he could have lost control of."

"Why didn't you report this earlier?" Inspector Finchley asked. "Are you telling us the truth?"

"Why would he lie?" I asked.

"For the attention. Some people enjoy involving themselves in drama." Inspector Finchley quirked an eyebrow at me.

"No! Not me. I keep my head down," the waiter said. "I was scared, sir. This job is important to me, and I can't afford to lose it. I thought they'd sort it out themselves. Besides, Sir Gerald got up after a second, brushed himself off, and they shook hands. I thought it was over."

"But it wasn't," I murmured. "Not with Sir Gerald turning up dead in my cellar."

"You can go," Inspector Finchley said to the waiter.

The waiter bolted away, shutting the door behind him.

Before we could digest this information, the door burst open, and Reginald Harcourt strode in. His expression was one of irritation.

Inspector Finchley jumped from his seat. "Is there something I can help you with, sir?"

"I should jolly well think so. How long must we wait?" Reginald asked. "I have an important engagement this evening, and I don't intend to miss it because you're slacking off."

"You can't leave. You need to answer our questions, Mr Harcourt," I said. "After all, a man is dead."

"That's quite enough, Miss Vale." Inspector Finchley bobbed about as if unsure whether to bow or curtsy.

For heaven's sake! Reginald was hardly a member of the royal family, so there was no need for all this sickly deference. What was the man hoping for, a knighthood?

Jacob stood and gestured to the chair opposite us. "Please, join us. This won't take long. We're gathering information to find out what happened to Sir Gerald."

"I know that!" Reginald eyed the chair with distaste but sat. "This is quite a party you have in here. Everyone getting involved, I see."

Inspector Finchley went to make the introductions, but Reginald stopped him. "I know everyone's name. Ask away. Let's get this torrid business dealt with so we can all carry on with our business."

"Tell us about your disagreement with Sir Gerald." I jumped in while Inspector Finchley flapped around like an old maid who'd exposed too much ankle on a public walk.

Reginald's lips twitched into a wry smile. "Disagreement? Which one are you referring to?"

"You admit to arguing with Sir Gerald?" Inspector Finchley finally remembered where his seat was and settled in, grabbing his notepad.

"Gerald and I were always at each other's throats. It was our dynamic, you might say. But if I'd wanted him dead, I'd have killed him a long time ago. The chap was infuriating, but he wasn't worth ruining this cricket event. Nothing will get in my way of a jolly good match. That was the focus for today. You always put on a splendid event, Miss Vale."

"That's kind of you." I raised an eyebrow. "Although that was an odd thing to say."

Reginald's brow furrowed. "What are you referring to?"

"I'm leading the questions." Inspector Finchley finally had himself under control. He even had his pencil the right way up.

"Be my guest," I said. "But don't you think Mr Harcourt should show more remorse? Even if he wasn't the best of friends with our victim."

"I was easing the mood. Attempting humour by saying the game was the most important matter," Reginald said with a small shrug. "That was lost on you. Some females have no mind for fun. Especially the older, unmarried ones."

Jacob's hand gently brushed against mine. It was a silent reminder to keep my composure in the face of bold rudeness.

"Very droll. What was the nature of your disagreement with Sir Gerald when you were on the cricket pitch?" I asked.

Inspector Finchley shuffled his chair forward to draw attention to himself.

Reginald sighed. "Gerald was smug. Arrogant. A hothead. But then, you'd know that if you'd spent five minutes with him. We often butted heads, usually about business. He had a knack for rubbing people the wrong way."

"Can you be more specific about your recent disagreement?" Inspector Finchley asked.

Reginald waved a hand dismissively. "It was trivial, and everyone heard us. He read the game wrong and didn't enjoy being shown up as a fool. And ... well, let me just say, the chap knows how to hold a grudge."

"About what?" I asked.

"There was lingering resentment over a property deal. It's been dealt with. I won the property, and he didn't. It was nothing worth killing over. As I said, we often debated, but business acumen always wins out. Is that all? I really must leave."

"One more question," I said.

Reginald glanced at Inspector Finchley, amusement glinting in his eyes. "I can tell who's in charge here. Very well, Miss Vale, since the cricket was so entertaining and I have high regard for this establishment, I'll allow it. What question do you have for me?"

"Inspector Finchley asked everyone without a solid alibi for the time of the murder to remain behind."

"Yes! Thank you, Miss Vale. That's enough. Mr Harcourt, please vouch for your whereabouts during the event. I have information here..." Inspector Finchley reviewed his notes, a flush of panic rising up his neck when he couldn't read his scrawled handwriting.

I'd have felt sorry for the man if he wasn't so irritating.

"Someone saw you leaving your table during the luncheon," Inspector Finchley said. "You disappeared for half an hour. Where did you go?"

"Ah, yes. True enough." Reginald adjusted his cufflinks. "It's rather embarrassing. A personal matter. Nothing to do with what happened to poor old Gerald."

"We won't gossip about your personal affairs," I said. "But we need to know where you went."

"Very well. I forgot my heart pills. I'm not sure they do me any good, but I always follow my doctor's orders. Rather than risk it, I walked home and picked them up."

"Can anyone vouch for you returning home?" Inspector Finchley asked.

"My maid. She saw me."

"Very good." Inspector Finchley flipped shut his notebook. "Thank you, Mr Harcourt. You're free to go."

Reginald rose, straightening his jacket. "I trust you'll keep me informed when you find the real culprit. Good day."

As the door closed behind him, I turned to Inspector Finchley. "You're letting him go? Just like that?"

Inspector Finchley scowled. "Mr Harcourt has an alibi, as I knew he would."

"You didn't even ask to see his pill bottle."

"It wasn't necessary."

"Reginald ran around the cricket pitch like a man half his age," I said. "There's nothing wrong with his heart!"

Jacob cleared his throat. "Veronica has a point, Inspector. You could check with Reginald's doctor and his maid."

Inspector Finchley's eyes narrowed. "I'm in charge of this investigation, not you. You had your chance to run things around here, and you blew it."

"Jacob was blown up in the line of duty and almost killed! That's quite a different matter," I said.

"There's no need to get hysterical." Inspector Finchley gestured at Jacob. "You need to take her in hand."

I drew in a sharp breath, and my fist clenched, but I restrained myself by sheer force of will. Making an enemy of this bumbling, small-minded inspector would only hinder my progress in solving this crime.

Inspector Finchley stood. "Miss Vale, I know you think you have the skills and experience to solve every crime in this city, but I'll give you some advice you should take in a sensible spirit. Stick to your obituaries. Luck will only carry you so far."

It took every ounce of restraint not to snap back. Instead, I met his glare with my own. "I'll keep an eye on Reginald Harcourt, Inspector. Even if you don't. Money and a title do nothing to impress me or cloud my judgement when solving a murder."

"Leave that fine gentleman alone! He comes from an excellent family and holds a prestigious position in the city. He also donates regularly to the Policeman's Fund."

I scoffed at him. "This is about money?"

"Of course not!"

"Then what is it? Don't think any of Reginald's prestige will rub off on you because you treat him like he's a pillar of the community," I said. "You grovel before these men, hoping to get a scrap of respect tossed your way. You're a fool. They're laughing at you behind your back."

"Veronica," Jacob cautioned, but I was too angry to hold my tongue.

Inspector Finchley inhaled sharply. "I respect those in positions of authority and show them the appropriate respect. That is called good manners. And you're no better. I saw you fawning over Lady M and Lady Valentine."

"Fawning! I have a sensible, adult relationship with Lady M. We respect each other."

Inspector Finchley sneered at me. "And I respect Mr Harcourt. As should you." With that, he turned and left the room, yelling for Sergeant Matthers to join him.

I let out an exasperated breath, pacing the length of the room. Jacob leaned back in his chair, his arms crossed, and his gaze steady as he watched me.

"I cannot believe him!" I hissed. "That man wouldn't recognise a killer if they confessed to his face. How did you deal with him when you worked together?"

Jacob tilted his head. "He has his moments, but he's a solid inspector."

"When he's not fawning over the higher-ups!" I stopped mid-stride. "Reginald practically danced across the cricket pitch, and yet we're supposed to believe he has a heart condition? It's absurd. And Inspector Finchley's poor questioning techniques were even more so. All he's concerned about is not having enough money in the Policeman's Fund for the next Christmas party."

Jacob's expression grew serious. "Inspector Finchley might have bought his story, but I'm guessing you're not planning to let it lie?"

"I don't care how many silver spoons Reginald Harcourt had in his mouth when he was born. If he's involved in Sir Gerald's murder, we shall find out."

Jacob moved to block my pacing, gently catching my arm. "Don't forget the waiter's story. Charles is just as suspicious. He has a solid motive for wanting Sir Gerald dead."

"I've forgotten none of it. There's more deception at this event than at a magician's show. It's a pity Inspector Finchley can't see that."

Jacob smiled. "Isn't that why you're here?"

I held his gaze, my resolve hardening, even as my anger faded. "I'll make sure the killer can't weasel their way out with charm and half-truths."

Jacob released my arm and gestured towards the door. "Well then, where do we start? You lead, and I'll follow."

I nodded, already forming a plan. Someone had lied to me, but I intended to uncover the truth.

Chapter 10

"Another gin fizz?" Cedric asked as he cleared the empty glasses off the bar, where I'd been sitting with Jacob for the last hour, formatting our next actions. Benji was curled by my feet, full of treats after spending so long with Cedric. The man adored dogs almost as much as I did.

"I should stick to tea if you wouldn't mind making me one, especially since it's getting late," I said.

"I'll have another half," Jacob said. "It's been one of those days."

"Having to deal with Inspector Finchley, you mean?" I asked.

Jacob's smile was rueful. "I understand why you think little of him."

"Naturally. Every time we meet, we clash. And his view on women is boorish."

"I agree. But Finchley has been in this business all his life. He knows a few things."

"All that means is he's seen nothing outside the world of law enforcement," I said. "How does that make for a well-rounded character? And a man too stubborn to accept help, no matter the source, is the wrong sort of chap to lead a murder investigation."

"Here's your tea," Cedric said. "I added a dash of sugar."

I nodded thanks as he set a cup on the bar. "Will you join us?"

"Thank you, but much like you, it's been a trying day. Finding a body in your cellar is the last thing you want," Cedric said. "And since we can't reopen until the police give me the nod, there's nothing much for me to do."

"You've been a sterling help," I said.

Cedric hesitated. "I am sorry about taking the money. Do ... do I still have a job?"

"You've made it clear you knew you were in the wrong, and having checked the books, I see where you've made repayments."

Cedric gulped.

"You are still landlord of the Jolly Cricketer. But the next time—"

"I promise it will never happen again."

I settled a stern glare on him. "In case temptation ever looms again, speak to me. I will help you."

"Thank you. I'm so grateful. You don't know how much this means to me."

"Have the rest of the evening off," I said. "The pub will soon reopen, and rather ghoulishly, murder brings in curious onlookers, so the place will soon be fit to bursting."

Cedric shuddered. "There's a grim thought. You know where everything is, so help yourself if you need anything else. I'll say goodnight."

He left the spare front door key on the bar, should I require it, then donned his coat and cap and headed outside for a smoke.

"Why are you smiling?" I asked Jacob. "Murder isn't something you enjoy. Not after all your years of dealing with criminals."

"Murder brings a light into your eyes."

I lightly swatted his arm. "Now you're the one being ghoulish. Although I admit, I spend an unnatural amount of time around the deceased. That's all part of the job."

"You enjoy it. And not because of the death, but what you achieve by solving an injustice. That always motivated me. Many people don't have the connections to solve their problems. They get ignored and left behind. That's where we come in."

"You can't say that about the chaps who played cricket here today," I said.

"Which is why we must be cautious," Jacob said. "These are men of influence. They know how to apply pressure to the police."

"It's a good job we aren't the police. There's a benefit to operating outside the parameters of the law."

"We won't do that. Not with our new business. Or Inspector Finchley will arrest you," Jacob said.

"With Lady M providing me with an open door to this investigation, we have our own source of influence," I said. "Even the most influential chap at this cricket match would be a fool to go up against her resources."

"Don't underestimate the power of a male ego," Jacob said. "Many of these men are new money and have made their fortunes in the city. They don't have the same level of respect for generational wealth."

"Then they'll learn the hard way. Lady M is not to be trifled with," I said. "And neither are we. With Inspector Finchley throwing up roadblocks, and his prejudice when dealing with influential city types, we need to ensure nothing is missed."

"We have plenty to keep us busy without prodding Inspector Finchley," Jacob said. "Eleanor's affair with the victim. Charles knowing about it. It must have been one of them."

"Charles is the obvious candidate," I said. "Although he can't keep a secret to save his life, so if he was the killer, he'd slip up and reveal himself."

"Charles assumed Eleanor told us everything to save herself," Jacob said. "And we know how ladies like to gossip."

"We're not all gossips!"

"There's no harm in it," Jacob said. "Over the years, unguarded talk has provided me with valuable information."

I leaned back as I cupped the hot tea. "Is there any way you can think of to sweeten Inspector Finchley? Without Ruby by my side, the option to flatter him into subservience is out of the question."

"I'll have a word and see if I can get through to him," Jacob said.

"I expect you had several less-than-complimentary words about me when I poked about in your investigations."

"I can't deny that," Jacob said with a wry smile. "Once Inspector Finchley has calmed, he'll realise you're an asset. And he remembers how effective you were when investigating the Swan Tavern murder."

"We solved the case for him! And you weren't even there to lend a hand." I involuntarily flinched and fell silent. Jacob had been away, looking into the mystery surrounding my father's death.

Jacob allowed the silence between us to stretch. Wretched man. He knew what an effective tactic it was.

"I know what you're doing," I finally said.

"Enjoying a quiet drink while discussing murder with my favourite person?"

I sighed, reaching down to rest a hand on Benji's soft head. He was always a comfort during trying times such as this.

"We don't have to talk about it," Jacob said. "We have plenty of other things to keep us occupied."

I stared into my cup of tea, my thoughts churning. Just when I thought life had settled, something reared up and caused drama. Would things always be this way? Was I destined to lead a life of uncertainty?

I finished my tea. If I lived quietly, ignoring the toil of reality, I'd grow bored. But perhaps I threw myself into new projects to avoid troubling home truths. My obituary writing. Volunteering at the dogs' home. Setting up a new shelter in another county, alongside a private investigation business. I loved what I did, but I filled my life with so many distractions to avoid difficult personal issues.

I drew in a steadying breath and focused on Jacob. "The last time we spoke, you were talking to people about what happened to my father. Is there any progress?"

Jacob took a long sip of his ale, his steady gaze not leaving mine. "It's not good news."

"Whatever news it is, let's get it out in the open," I said. "I've been cowardly, shying from this business."

"It's not cowardly. Your father died in sad circumstances. You've been protecting yourself and the rest of your family. There's no shame in that."

"For me, there is. Did you find out what happened?" My breath lodged in my throat, and my words came out choked.

"No. My leads have gone cold."

"Such as they were," I said. "My apologies. That was unkind."

"There's no need to apologise," Jacob said. "You've been under tremendous pressure keeping this a secret. Although I don't think you should."

"Let's not go round in that unpleasant circle again, shall we? I'm not telling my mother or Matthew until I know for certain what happened."

"I don't agree, but I'll respect your wishes." Jacob pressed his lips together then nodded. "I thought I was onto something. A friend of a friend claims to have seen your father. There were even photographs."

"Seen? Just before he died, you mean?"

"No. After he died."

"That makes no sense," I said. "When one falls or jumps off a cliff, the sea carries you away. That's why Beachy Head is a popular place for such an unfortunate action. There was no body, but we know what happened."

"Which is why I became suspicious of the evidence," Jacob said. "I was investigating the manner of your father's death. Whether it was by his hand or because he fell foul of a villain."

"Exactly. That was your focus. Were you being fed lies?"

"One man began talking about payment. I researched his background and discovered he'd been involved in several conspiracies to defraud. He'd got away with his activities but had gained a reputation."

"Why didn't you learn that as soon as you questioned him?" I asked.

"He changed his name and moved to a different part of the country. He even got himself a forged passport. It was only through extensive digging and using my contacts that I discovered the truth. After that, I realised I was chasing a lie. And that was unfair on you and your family." Jacob held my hand. "It was an error, and I'm sorry for causing you concern."

I gulped back the threat of tears. "It's hard to accept such a joy-filled, larger-than-life man would find life too difficult to go on, but that's what happened."

"Yes, I believe you're right," Jacob said softly.

My breath came out shaky, feeling annoyance and relief. I'd never reached a satisfactory conclusion as to what I'd tell my family if this revelation was true. At least now, I didn't need to concern myself. We'd live with the sad fact that my father had found life too difficult to continue.

"Well, now that business is over," I said, "we can get on with things."

"Why not take time to think this over?"

"Thinking achieves nothing. Action does," I said. "And while I appreciate your help in dealing with Inspector Finchley and his old-fashioned ways, you are required in Margate."

"The new office can wait," Jacob said. "I want to spend time with you. I can help with this investigation. Don't you need an extra pair of hands, what with Ruby disappearing?"

"Wretched Ruby," I said. "She must turn up soon."

"With Lady M on the case and you chasing her down, if she's hiding, she won't for much longer," Jacob said.

"Even if Ruby doesn't resurface soon, I need you in Margate. We have fresh cases coming in. And there's a site you need to investigate for the new dogs' home."

Jacob nodded. "There is an interesting case that's come across my desk. A possible financial scam. Lots of big players in the mix."

"And I see from the gleam in your eye that's piqued your interest," I said. "Go to Margate. We have a plan. You have several days to work on this case and the other open files, and then I'll join you on the weekend. You can show me the location of the dogs' home, and then we can enjoy some rare time off."

"Veronica Vale doesn't know how to have time off," Jacob said. "The last time we were in Margate on holiday, you found time to solve yet another murder."

"With your esteemed help, naturally." I leaned forward and kissed his cheek. "Now, let's finish making plans, shall we? We have so much to do."

"If you bring that dog in here, the least you could do is teach it to behave." Bob lurked by my desk, a scowl on his dour face, his cheeks unshaven.

"If you're referring to my impeccably trained Benji, I can assure you, he knows exactly how to behave. Especially around scoundrels. Sometimes, he bites them." I'd been so absorbed in finishing the pile of obituaries on my desk that I hadn't noticed Benji disappear.

It was unlike him. I checked the time and realised I'd missed giving him his mid-morning snack. He must be hungry. And a hungry dog was a motivated one.

"My corned beef sandwich is missing!" Bob said. "Your dog stole it."

"Benji dislikes corned beef. It upsets his stomach." I looked around and discovered Benji dashing out of Uncle Harry's office, clearly having gone to the easiest target for a delicious snack.

"There he is! And he's eating something." Bob jabbed a finger at Benji. "I want my lunch."

"You could retrieve it once it's been digested," I said. "Although I suspect it won't be appetising by then. However, Benji does not steal. He has manners. Unlike many of the men around here. Now, if you'll excuse me—"

"I will not excuse you. You're going out and getting me my lunch. And you're paying for it."

"What's going on out here?" Uncle Harry emerged from his office, his tie slung over one shoulder and his top button undone.

"She's being stubborn again," Bob said. "She's refusing to give me information about the murder at her pub."

"You absolute liar! You were bothering me about your missing sandwich. You're a dreadful investigative reporter if you can't solve such a simple puzzle."

"I know exactly what four-legged beast took my lunch," Bob said. "And I want those details on the murder. You don't get to write the story just because you own the place."

"Veronica always provides you with the information you need to write excellent stories," Uncle Harry said. He reached into his trouser pocket, pulled out a few coins, and handed them to Bob. "Take a walk and buy yourself a sandwich. You can't write a good story if you're hungry."

Bob glowered at me as he pocketed the money. He turned and strode out of the office, muttering to himself.

"I took it." Uncle Harry had lowered his voice. "I slept here last night, and there was nothing in the fridge when I got up. I saw Bob put his lunch in there, so I snuck out the sandwich. I meant to replace it, but I lost track of time. Sorry if he caused you trouble."

I chuckled to myself. "Bob is a continual thorn in my side, but one I'm well used to."

"He picks on you. It's not fair," Uncle Harry said. "But make sure you tell him everything about the murder at the Jolly Cricketer. Since you were there, we've got the inside scoop and eyewitnesses."

"I assure you, Bob will have the facts," I said. The telephone on my desk rang, and I answered it.

"It's Sergeant Matthers. I've had word that Eleanor Pembroke has requested a meeting with Inspector Finchley. She's heard on the grapevine that her affair is becoming public knowledge."

"And she's concerned we'll look at her as the guilty party?" I was already collecting my things.

"I reckon so," Sergeant Matthers said. "She'll be here in an hour. Inspector Finchley told me not to say anything, but you're involved, so it's only right you're here."

"You're an excellent fellow, Sergeant. I'll be with you shortly."

We said our goodbyes, and I set down the telephone.

"Progress on the case?" Uncle Harry asked.

"A nervous suspect," I said. "Fear not, I'll record everything and hand it to Bob, so he gets the prime byline. Perhaps by the end of the day, we'll have ourselves a confession."

Chapter 11

I'd been waiting for five minutes in the sterile reception area of the police station after Sergeant Matthers's telephone call. A young man was making a kerfuffle and seemed set to continue until a stern stare from me quietened him and he mumbled an apology.

"Veronica! Sorry to keep you." Sergeant Matthers gestured for me to follow as he held the door open. "Eleanor's quite tearful. We needed to find a female police officer to observe the interview and ensure its proper conduct."

"I'd have been happy to do that job," I said.

"I suggested that to Inspector Finchley, and he bit my head off." Sergeant Matthers led me along a plain corridor towards the interview room. "I reminded him of your experience and how helpful you've been to us, but he got red in the face, and the yelling started."

"He'll do himself a mischief if he gets so het up over such trivial matters," I said. "He knows I'm not going away, so he may as well utilise my skills. If he doesn't, I'll have to speak to Lady M and mention what a bother he's being."

Sergeant Matthers chuckled. "It's best you don't. He's got Detective Chief Inspector Taylor breathing down his neck on this one. He knew the deceased gentleman. They've played cricket together at the pub, and he doesn't want the club's reputation sullied by a murder. Especially not a murder involving someone so prominent."

"What a surprise to hear Detective Chief Inspector Taylor enjoys hobnobbing with the wealthy types," I said. "But if we're to wrap this up quickly, Inspector Finchley must let me get stuck in."

Sergeant Matthers winced. "He told me you're to sit in the corner and not make a sound."

I patted Sergeant Matthers's arm as we stopped by a closed door. "I make no guarantees."

Sergeant Matthers opened the door. Eleanor sat at a table opposite Inspector Finchley, a young female officer beside her.

Inspector Finchley's face was like thunder, and it only darkened when he saw me. He made no introductions, simply pointed to a chair in the corner of the room. I suspected he'd selected it himself, as it was a most uncomfortable seat.

"Now everyone's here." Inspector Finchley gave me a pointed look. "We can begin the interview. If you're feeling up to it, Mrs Pembroke?"

"Eleanor, please." Her eyes were red-rimmed, and she kept dabbing delicately at her nose with an immaculately trimmed lace handkerchief. "I can manage, Inspector. I'm so ashamed to be involved in this dreadful business."

"We'll make this as easy on you as we can, but we need the facts to find out what happened to Sir Gerald."

"Yes, of course. That is why I'm here," Eleanor said. "I didn't want to deceive you at our first meeting, but I ... I concealed something from you."

"Go on," Inspector Finchley said.

"I was more intimately acquainted with Gerald than I led you to believe," Eleanor said.

I pressed my lips together, forcing myself not to ask a question.

"How close were you and Sir Gerald?" Inspector Finchley asked.

"I've ... oh, this is embarrassing. I've been having difficulties in my marriage, and Gerald was helpful. He supported me. And he listened to me. He was a marvellous man."

"Was your relationship of an intimate nature?" Inspector Finchley asked, his gaze darting to the floor as he asked the question.

Eleanor dabbed at her eyes with her handkerchief. "I fell for his charms. Being a married woman doesn't mean you aren't lonely. I'm mortified about what I did. I take my marriage vows seriously."

I arched an eyebrow and caught Sergeant Matthers's gaze. He appeared to be more sympathetic than I was. Eleanor was only revealing her affair with Sir Gerald because her husband disclosed it to us. She knew concealing the affair made her look guilty after her claim she barely knew the man.

"Would you like a moment to compose yourself?" Inspector Finchley asked.

"No, let's get this over with," Eleanor said. "For all my husband's genial nature when in public, he isn't kind to me. Not only am I lonely, but I'm scared to be in his company."

"Has Mr Pembroke ever raised a hand to you?" Inspector Finchley asked.

"Not yet, but he has a terrible temper," Eleanor said. "He found out what was going on with Gerald and pressured me to end things. He threatened to ruin me if I didn't finish it."

"If you don't mind me saying—"

"We do, Miss Vale," Inspector Finchley interrupted. "Or should I remind you of your place in this situation?"

Eleanor looked at me, her expression curious. "Inspector Finchley mentioned you'd attend this interview. I don't mind. My understanding is you're close friends with Lady M."

"We have a solid acquaintance," I said. "And she's keen on knowing what happened to Sir Gerald. As am I."

"If Lady M trusts you, then so do I," Eleanor said. "She's an excellent lady of the highest standing. If you have a question, please ask."

"With Inspector Finchley's permission," I said sweetly.

"Get on with it," Inspector Finchley said.

I had to grab this opportunity, so I cut straight to the point. "If you don't mind me saying, you have a motive for wanting Sir Gerald out of your life."

"What would that be?" Eleanor asked. "I loved the man."

"You must also love the lifestyle provided for you by your husband. The central London home. The jewels.

The house in Italy. You wouldn't want to risk that being taken away by a scandal," I said.

"If I wanted money, Gerald would have provided that," Eleanor said. "He was wealthier than Charles. And he had a long-standing reputation in the city. Besides, if I'd intended to kill anyone, it would have been my cold, cruel husband." She let out a little sob and clutched the handkerchief against her chest.

"When you've quite finished upsetting Mrs Pembroke, I'd like to continue, so the dear lady can go home," Inspector Finchley said.

I studied Eleanor as Inspector Finchley resumed his questioning. I didn't believe this act. She knew the tears would soften him towards her. She was here to save face. And she had an excellent motive.

There was no guarantee Sir Gerald wanted anything more than an affair. If she lost Charles because of her salacious behaviour, she'd be left with nothing. Eleanor could have acted out of panic, especially if Sir Gerald was pressuring her or threatening to reveal their relationship. Maybe he'd been the one planning to ruin her.

"Could you remind me of your alibi for the afternoon of the murder?" Inspector Finchley asked.

"I was with my sister," Eleanor said. "We barely left the table. Well, only for a few minutes. My sister took a brief walk because she finds crowds tiring, but neither of us had the opportunity to meet Gerald."

When tawdry love affairs were concerned, the couple grabbed any opportunity to snatch a kiss. A dark cellar, where they wouldn't be seen, was the perfect meeting place.

"Thank you for being so honest with us," Inspector Finchley said. "I'll be in touch if I have more questions."

"Before I go, Inspector, I'd like to know what you plan on doing next. Gerald was definitely murdered, wasn't he?"

"We believe so," Inspector Finchley said.

"Does that mean you'll pursue my husband?" Eleanor pressed a hand on Inspector Finchley's arm. "As I said, he has a dreadful temper."

How clever of Eleanor. She was setting up Charles to take the fall for something she could have done.

"Don't worry yourself about that," Inspector Finchley said.

"I must! Is it even safe for me to go home?"

Inspector Finchley hesitated. "Perhaps you could stay with your sister?"

"Finella lives with us," Eleanor said. "She's a wonderful support. I'm sure if she's there, I have nothing to worry about."

"I'm happy to hear that." Inspector Finchley stood and opened the door. "Let me see you out. But please, do telephone if you have any concerns."

I looked at Sergeant Matthers as soon as they had left the room and the door was closed. "How unfortunate for Charles. Everyone thinks he's guilty. After that performance, I'm not so certain he is."

—*ele*—

After Eleanor's tear-soaked interview, Inspector Finchley vanished. No doubt because he knew

I intended to question him and formalise the investigation's next steps.

After waiting and requesting a meeting with him, I realised he intended to slight me all day. A telephone call to Lady M would soon resolve that rude behaviour.

I returned to work and outlined two obituaries. My telephone rang. I answered, unsurprised and a trifle amused to hear Inspector Finchley on the other end of the line. Lady M had been most efficient.

"I don't appreciate you getting me in trouble," he said.

"Whatever have I done now?" I asked.

"You spoke to Lady M. She's been bending my ear for ten minutes, insisting you remain a part of this investigation. I told her you were involved!"

"I'm hardly involved. You sat me in a corner like a naughty schoolgirl."

"You asked a question. And by doing so, you upset Eleanor."

"Eleanor fooled you," I said. "Don't let a woman's tears deceive you."

"I'm not as green as I am cabbage-looking," Inspector Finchley retorted.

I stifled a laugh. "I would describe you as parsnip-like, Inspector. Does that mean you don't believe Eleanor's story?"

"I'm aware she pointed our attention towards her husband, possibly to distract us. She's an intelligent woman. Intelligence can turn to cunning. Especially in the fairer sex."

"Well done for keeping such an open mind, Inspector," I said. "Is this telephone call to apologise, or do we have more work to do?"

"We are not working together. I'm allowing you to be a silent observer in this investigation. Lady M has influence, but so do I."

"In that case, what shall I silently observe next?"

Inspector Finchley huffed out a breath. "Charles Pembroke is arriving at the station at six o'clock tonight. After everything his wife said, he needs another talking-to."

"Is that an invitation to join you?"

"If you must. But remember the rules."

"And you remember yours," I said, "or Lady M won't be happy. And next time, she may pay you a visit."

He muttered something unintelligible, barely said goodbye, and ended the telephone call.

With a smile on my face, I settled back to my work.

Soon enough, I was waving goodbye to Uncle Harry and heading back to the police station. This time, I took Benji. Inspector Finchley would have to sneeze and splutter his way through this interview.

We were in the same interview room, and I'd been given the same uncomfortable chair. Sergeant Matthers sat with Inspector Finchley, sitting opposite Charles.

Charles looked perplexed as I settled myself. "Still doing your private eye stuff, eh? Thought you'd be bored by now."

"It's easier to have her here," Inspector Finchley grumbled. "Then I don't have to repeat the information. Of course, you can request that the untrained civilian be excluded."

"I'm very much trained. And first-hand information is always welcome," I said.

"Since your pub was where old Gerald met a sticky wicket, you want to know what happened, and I have no issue with that." Charles turned back to Inspector Finchley. "But I must say, I didn't appreciate the order to show up for questioning. What's this about?"

Inspector Finchley began the interview and proceeded with the questions. "We spoke to another guest who attended the cricket event. She gave us cause for concern about your behaviour."

"A female! I can imagine who that was. What did my loving wife tell you?" Charles's tone was sharp.

"I didn't say it was your wife," Inspector Finchley said.

"Eleanor has no love for me. I've already told you about her affair. You can't believe a word that strumpet says."

"Eleanor provided us with some insight, but we have evidence from another source," I said. "A witness claims to have seen you in an altercation with Sir Gerald."

"If anyone told you that, Eleanor put them up to it. She probably charmed them into lying. She has a way about her most men find irresistible. I include myself in that. At least, I used to."

"You're denying the fight?" I asked.

"Well, no! We had a few words."

"Talk us through it," Inspector Finchley said.

"It was nothing," Charles replied. "High spirits and too much to drink."

"How could you be civil to a man who was having an affair with your wife?" I asked.

Charles bristled and took his time adjusting his tie. "My business connections and reputation in the city are far more important than a passing fancy I made the mistake of marrying. Eleanor will soon be long gone, but my career will span decades. I will not have my reputation sullied by her mistakes."

"I'm sorry to say, sir," Inspector Finchley said, "but a waiter witnessed you having a violent altercation with Sir Gerald shortly before he died. You punched him."

I nodded slightly, impressed Inspector Finchley hadn't backed down from a man he considered his better.

Charles sighed heavily. "Very well. Things got heated. I shouldn't have let myself get so angry, but Gerald was making snide comments about Eleanor. He wasn't a kind man. I lost my temper and defended Eleanor's honour. I shouldn't have wasted my time. And I hurt my hand."

"Remind us again of your movements that afternoon," Inspector Finchley said.

"I was watching the match or at the bar getting a drink. You have that on record."

"Did you meet Sir Gerald in the cellar?" Inspector Finchley asked.

"Why would I? Gerald humiliated me. But I know he's not to blame. Eleanor would have chased after him. Gerald wasn't married, and Eleanor's beguiling ways did the rest. I was angry with the man but understood why he fell for her. Her charm is captivating. Thankfully, I've seen the truth."

"You must understand how this gives you a powerful motive for wanting Sir Gerald dead," I said.

"Maybe it does, but their affair had been going on for months. Why would I choose to act now? And in such a public arena?" Charles asked.

"Because Sir Gerald's disparaging comments about your wife pushed you over the edge," I said.

"That's quite enough, Miss Vale," Inspector Finchley said. "Mr Pembroke, we'll need to double-check your movements. This situation requires thorough investigation."

"You'll find nothing to connect me to this crime," Charles said. "I have an excellent reputation in the business community, and I wouldn't destroy that because of my wife's indiscretion."

After a few more questions, Inspector Finchley escorted Charles to the door, and he was free to leave.

"Inspector, may I enquire what your next move is in this investigation?" I asked.

"No, you may not. I've had enough of your snooping. You have a disagreeable inability to follow basic orders. I told you to stay quiet. Good evening, Miss Vale." Inspector Finchley strode away.

"Irritating chap," I muttered to Benji.

"He's had a long day." There was a note of apology in Sergeant Matthers's voice. "He got hauled over the coals by the chief for two different cases."

"That's hardly my fault. Perhaps I should offer my services on the other case to ensure he makes progress."

Sergeant Matthers chuckled as he led me to the exit. "Only if you want to make him your sworn enemy."

"What a terrifying thought. Good evening, Sergeant." Once I was outside, I stood for a moment with Benji. "Let's take a brisk walk. Blow that frustrating man out of my hair while we ponder Charles's answers."

Benji's tail wagged in agreement, and we weaved towards the nearest park, doing our best to avoid the worst of the foot traffic and busy roads.

We walked in companionable silence for several minutes until Benji slowed, his hackles lifting, and a low growl rumbling from his throat.

I didn't look around. Benji's instincts were never wrong where trouble was concerned. Instead, I veered off the main path and led us behind a large tree and crouched with Benji.

A few seconds later, hurried, uneven footsteps approached, one foot making an odd, solid thunk every time it hit the ground. A man sped past.

I gave Benji a signal, and he bolted after the man like a rocket. Benji leapt, slamming into our pursuer's back and sending him sprawling.

The man yelped, rolling over, only to freeze when he saw Benji's bared teeth hovering inches from his face.

I dashed out from behind the tree and stopped in my tracks, my eyes widening. "Dirk!"

Chapter 12

I held out a hand to help Dirk up from the dirt.

He waved away my offer. "I landed in mud when Benji took me down. You don't need to get dirty, too."

Benji backed away when he realised there was no immediate threat to my safety, though he still eyed Dirk warily.

"Good boy," I said, scratching behind Benji's ears. "You did exactly what I asked you to do."

By this time, Dirk was on his feet, brushing his palms against his thighs. "It was my fault. I should have hailed you. I was out of breath, though. My lungs haven't been the same since serving."

I studied him carefully. Dirk was dishevelled from his fall, and tension radiated off him. He kept glancing around as if worried someone was watching.

"Is there some kind of trouble?" I asked.

"You always were the sharp one." He looked over his shoulder again. "Let's keep walking. We don't want to be spotted together."

"Goodness! You make it sound as if you're an undercover spy. The Germans didn't turn you, I hope?"

"Perish the thought." Dirk checked his pockets to make sure nothing had fallen out then gestured along the path. "There's a decent café a short walk from here that stays open late. Let me buy you a coffee, and I'll explain everything."

After a second's hesitation, I nodded. Why had Dirk sought me out? We knew of each other's reputations in journalism, but I wouldn't call us close friends. Perhaps he was looking for an angle on the murder. Or he'd uncovered a clue he wished to share with me.

Dirk kept to the shadows as we walked through the park. He also glanced around frequently, as if expecting to see someone following us.

"Was there something you wanted to speak to me about?" I asked.

"Let's wait until we're inside," Dirk said.

"You're acting most suspiciously. I assure you, if anyone approaches us with ill intent, Benji will see them off."

"I've no doubt. He's an excellent dog," Dirk said. "The perfect protector."

"He's had plenty of experience," I said. "I occasionally get accused of being rash with my behaviour. Benji ensures I don't come to a sticky end."

"We all need a Benji," Dirk said with a faint smile.

"I know of an excellent dog rescue shelter, if you're interested."

"I have neither the funds nor a place to house such a fine fellow."

By this time, we'd reached the other side of the park. Dirk led us to a modest café, brightly lit and bustling with a few late-night patrons.

We entered, and I was pleased that Benji could join us. Dirk ordered two coffees and a bowl of water for Benji, who gratefully lapped it up.

Dirk deliberately chose a table at the back of the café, away from the other customers, so we could talk without being overheard.

I settled into my seat and waited for him to begin. The silence stretched out, but I said nothing.

"It's a dreadful business, what happened at the Jolly Cricketer," Dirk finally said once the server delivered our coffees.

"I assumed that was what you wanted to talk about," I said. "I'm afraid you've missed the boat if you're looking to submit an exclusive story. The London Times is all over this case."

"No, that doesn't interest me," Dirk said. "I want to know what happened, but I'm not looking for an exclusive. And I know you well enough. You'd never reveal information that would damage an investigation. Rumour has it, you're making a name for yourself with private investigations."

"Those rumours are true." I sipped my coffee. "If it's not the murder, why did you wish to speak to me?"

Dirk leaned closer. "I'm in a spot of bother. The police want to question me."

"That's nothing to concern yourself with. They've spoken to everybody who was at the charity event. Including me. For the briefest of moments, the foolish inspector leading the investigation tried to make me a suspect!"

Dirk choked on a laugh. "Is the man a buffoon?"

"He does his best to appear as one," I said. "Inspector Finchley is competent enough, but he comes from the old school of policing, and he has outdated beliefs. He's no fan of outsiders intruding on his investigations. But intrude I must! I won't have an unsolved murder lingering over my pub."

"You'll talk sense into him," Dirk said. "And I'm not concerned about speaking to the police. They've already interviewed me."

"Then what's the problem?" I asked.

"They ... they think I could be involved." His eyes widened a fraction as he studied my reaction. "And to set the record straight, I'm not. I was there, of course, but I was covering the cricket match. That was my only interest."

I sighed. "Inspector Finchley will always look at the outsider. You don't fit in with the esteemed social circle, so you're a target."

"It's a little more than that," Dirk said. "I wasn't on the best of terms with the victim."

"How did you know Sir Gerald? I mean no offence, but we both know freelance journalism is hard to make a living from, especially since the war, so you won't have attended the same parties."

"Don't I know it! It's a hand-to-mouth existence. If I didn't have such a love for the written word and sport, I'd have given up," Dirk said.

"I'll ask Uncle Harry for help. You have an excellent way with words. I'm not a sports fan, but I always enjoy your copy."

"That's kind of you, but if the police have their way, I won't be writing any more words. Except from behind bars."

"It can't be that serious," I said. "Why weren't you on good terms with Sir Gerald?"

Dirk stared into his cup of coffee. "We were both cricket-obsessed, so our paths would cross at matches. I once made the mistake of asking him for a quote."

"And he didn't appreciate the intrusion?"

"He told me to get a proper job. He said I was a hack and my career choice was a joke."

"Oh dear. Why ever would he say that?"

"I overheard Sir Gerald at the same match, bragging about a business deal he'd pulled off and the bonus he'd get. He saw the unimpressed expression on my face and pulled me up. In response, I may have said: when you know the right people, you'll always be a success."

"You disparaged his career in front of his friends, so he did the same to you?"

"That's the size of it. After that, we ignored each other," Dirk said. "I still went to the cricket matches, much like him, but we pretended the other didn't exist."

"Inspector Finchley learned of this disagreement, so he thinks you have a motive for wanting Sir Gerald dead?"

"It's absurd! But Inspector Finchley is making this into a problem," Dirk said. "Sir Gerald won't be the first toff to mock my career, and they're all still alive. That lot don't understand the skill it takes to put together a finely tuned piece of content. Sometimes, making cricket matches sound exciting isn't easy."

"The same goes for obituaries." I tapped my fingers against my cup. "It's a vague motive, at best."

"But it's one Inspector Finchley is interested in," Dirk said. "After my initial interview, I thought that would be the end of it. But then I received a summons to return for further questioning. I panicked. I thought when I got to the police station, they'd arrest me, and I'd never get out."

"You didn't attend your second interview?"

"I didn't. If I'm accused of this crime, I can't defend myself. I haven't got two pennies to rub together. And with Sir Gerald's money feeding the prosecution, I'd be a goner. An innocent man charged."

"It would never come to that," I said. "Inspector Finchley has his moments of stubborn-headed nincompoopery, but he wouldn't charge an innocent man."

"He's keen on closing this case quickly," Dirk said. "I heard mutterings about the chief inspector wanting a swift resolution. With me behind bars, there's your resolution! Even if it's the wrong one."

I shook my head, annoyed by Inspector Finchley's behaviour once again. Dirk struck me as a level-headed chap. He'd served his country loyally, and after returning from the war, he'd found joy by following his passion for sports and writing. Few men could attest to doing that.

"What about your alibi?" I asked.

"That's another problem," Dirk said. "When the cricket match ended, I left everyone to their food and headed home to write the article. I came back not long before Cedric found Sir Gerald."

"Someone must have seen you at home," I said. "Your wife? Or does she work?"

"I live on my own. Truth be told, it's a lonely existence. I had a girl who waited for me during the war, but when I came back with my injury, she wanted none of it." He leaned down and rapped his knuckles against his lower leg.

Benji's ears pricked, and he sniffed Dirk's leg.

"Oh! I didn't realise you'd been so badly wounded," I said. "Is the entire leg gone?"

"From the knee down. I'm used to it," Dirk said. "And I'm hoping to get an upgrade. They do amazing things with prosthetics. They're not cheap, though."

"Any woman worthy of you won't mind that injury," I said. "It's the character that makes the man."

"Then I've been talking to the wrong ladies," Dirk said. "As soon as they find out I'm not whole, they scarper. One girl even said my false leg made her feel sick. It's not that bad!"

"It most definitely isn't." I felt annoyed on his behalf.

Dirk sighed. "I'll just have to settle for a life on my own."

"We'll have none of that. I'm assuming everything else works?"

Dirk's cheeks flushed. "Of course it does!"

"You clearly have a brain, you're in excellent physical shape, and you're carving a niche for yourself in a career most people never achieve. Times are tough at the moment, but things will improve."

His smile was rueful. "I don't suppose you know any open-minded ladies who wouldn't mind a man missing a part of himself?"

"There is someone who would be charmed by you," I said, "but she's currently off on an adventure."

"That's a pity," Dirk said. "Perhaps I should set my sights on an older woman of influence. That Lady M and her friend at the cricket match, perhaps? I suppose they're not looking for a bit of rough?"

I chortled.

Dirk's gaze shot to the window, and he stood with a jerk. "How did they find me?"

I looked around to see three policemen peering through the window. One of them was Inspector Finchley.

"I've got to go!" Dirk was backing away, panic written all over his face.

"Stay and talk to them," I said. "We can clear this up together. I'm happy to vouch for your character."

Benji whined, sensing the tension.

"You don't understand. They'll arrest me!" Dirk turned and bolted towards the back of the café.

I threw down some coins and charged after him with Benji close at my heels.

"Veronica Vale!" Inspector Finchley bellowed my name as he slammed open the café door. "What are you doing with our prime suspect?"

The other customers stopped talking and stared at me.

I hesitated by the door Dirk had fled through, stepping back as Inspector Finchley's men rushed past. "Please don't tell me you're wasting time pursuing Dirk as a suspect?"

"You've gone too far!" Inspector Finchley radiated anger as he marched towards me. "Not only are you poking your nose into my case, but you're consorting with the suspects! What did you tell him? Trying to get him off this charge, I assume?"

I resisted the urge to tut. "Dirk Somerville is a respectable journalist."

"He's a hack," Inspector Finchley spat. "He sells lurid tales to the gutter press to make a quick penny. Lies about influential figures. All scandalous and false. He's lucky no one has sued him yet."

I blocked the door, preventing Inspector Finchley from following Dirk. "Dirk admitted he's struggling with his career, but that has nothing to do with this case."

"Don't think I won't push you out of the way," Inspector Finchley growled.

Benji snarled, causing Inspector Finchley to falter in his efforts to get past.

"Dirk won't get far. I'm sure you're aware of his leg injury," I said.

"Of course I am! That's why I must speak to him again."

"Inspector, as painful as this is for you to accept, I'm involved in this investigation. I demand to know what Dirk losing his limb has to do with this murder?"

"I don't have time for this. Step aside!"

"Answer me, and I will. Dirk admitted he wasn't on the best of terms with Sir Gerald, but he told me they'd smoothed over their differences."

"Then you know nothing," Inspector Finchley said with a sneer. "Dirk despised Sir Gerald. He was working on a story that would have ruined him."

"What story? Not about the charity match, surely?"

Inspector Finchley's expression turned smug. "Ah, the oh-so-clever Veronica Vale is in the dark for once. How disappointing for you."

Benji growled again, and I crossed my arms, arching an eyebrow at Inspector Finchley.

The café door opened, and one of the other policemen appeared. "We got him!"

"Excellent work. You have all the clues now." Inspector Finchley smirked at me. "Surely you can figure it out."

I gritted my teeth. "Please, enlighten me."

"Dirk was gathering evidence to discredit Sir Gerald's career. Sir Gerald confronted him at the charity match, and Dirk had the perfect weapon to hand. We suspected a cricket bat was the murder weapon, but—"

"Oh, my!" I gasped. "You think Dirk clubbed Sir Gerald to death with his wooden leg?"

Chapter 13

After Inspector Finchley's shocking accusation that Dirk committed the heinous crime using his false leg, I'd been quick to follow the police back to the station.

Inspector Finchley refused me entry to his vehicle, claiming only authorised personnel were permitted inside. What nonsense. It left me no choice but to hotfoot it to the nearest taxi with Benji and demand they follow the police. It was all very dramatic.

No matter what Inspector Finchley said, I refused to be shut out. And he was wrong about Dirk. As usual, Inspector Finchley wasn't engaging his brain. He'd found a convenient way to pin this crime on an outsider, and he was sticking with it.

He feared the loss of his job and his reputation far more than he feared an injustice occurring. That was where I came in. I wouldn't let this matter rest until I uncovered the truth. And the truth was not that Dirk Somerville was a killer.

Benji paced beside me as we waited for an update. I had to remain in the reception area again.

I wished Ruby were here. I needed her light-hearted nature and sense of fun to brighten this tense situation. It was most impractical of her to disappear when I needed her the most.

The door leading into the main station opened, and Sergeant Matthers poked his head out. "I told Inspector Finchley you wouldn't go home, no matter how long he ignored you."

"I'll stay all night if I must," I replied. "What is going on?"

"I've only got a minute. I told the inspector I'd get him a brew." Sergeant Matthers hurried over. "He's found evidence that makes Dirk look guilty."

"Inspector Finchley mentioned a story Dirk had put together. Some scandal on Sir Gerald?"

"Dirk was writing an expose. We don't know the exact ins and outs, but we're questioning Dirk to find out more."

"Where did you learn this information?" I asked.

"Dirk's landlady let us into his lodgings," he said. "We looked through some notepads and found the information. Dirk was investigating Sir Gerald's affairs."

"His affair with Eleanor?"

"There was no mention of Eleanor in the notes," Sergeant Matthers said. "If Dirk's research is accurate, the information would have ruined Sir Gerald. There are notes about suspicious business practices and concealing funds."

"But surely, if Sir Gerald realised this scandal was about to surface, he'd have wanted Dirk dead, not the other way around."

"Inspector Finchley believes they argued. There was a set-to, and Sir Gerald came off worse."

"Inspector Finchley must have checked Dirk's alibi. Someone would have seen him at the time the murder took place," I said.

"We know Dirk left the cricket match and returned home," Sergeant Matthers said. "So far, we have no witnesses."

"Only because of Inspector Finchley's lack of thoroughness. There must have been an eyewitness who saw Dirk leave the luncheon," I insisted. "He couldn't have done it if he was at home."

"We'll keep investigating, but at the moment, it's not looking good for Dirk."

"But consider the practicalities. If he used his false leg as the murder weapon, how would Dirk have managed such a punishing blow?" I asked. "He'd have been balancing on one leg! Swinging the false limb would have caused him to fall."

"If a concussion or injury hindered Sir Gerald, it would have given Dirk time to remove his leg and use it," Sergeant Matthers said. "We've taken the leg, and we're inspecting for damage and evidence of blood."

"How long will those tests take?" My worry mounted. Inspector Finchley seemed determined to pin this murder on Dirk.

"It'll be a day or two. And nothing will get done this evening," Sergeant Matthers said. He glanced over his shoulder. "I should get back. But before I do, I wanted to ask about Ruby. Is she back yet?"

"No. I was just thinking about her," I said.

Sergeant Matthers shifted from foot to foot. "I didn't want to say anything, so as not to worry you, but I was looking through the list of unidentified bodies."

My heart flip-flopped, launched into my throat, and then dropped into my chest, beating double-time. "Sergeant, are you suggesting Ruby could be one of those bodies?"

"No! At least, I sincerely hope not," he said. "We hold unidentified bodies at a central base, so I haven't seen them. But accurate descriptions are sent to local stations to see if we can connect any of the bodies with missing person cases."

I swallowed hard, trying to dislodge the lump in my throat. "And one body sounds like it could be Ruby?"

"I ... I believe so," he said. "I didn't want to worry you, but I thought you should know."

"Where is this body?"

"At the new mortuary on Hamburg Street."

"We need to go there. Immediately."

"I thought you'd say that," Sergeant Matthers said. "Give me five minutes. I need to make an excuse to leave that Inspector Finchley will believe."

I sank into a seat and wrapped my arms around Benji. It couldn't be my dear Ruby. But I had to know for sure.

What if something dreadful had happened? She could be impetuous and didn't always consider the danger in certain situations. No. Ruby had flights of fancy, but she was clever.

What about an accident?

I shook my head, forcing the panicked thoughts away. I wouldn't let my mind shove me off track and into fantasyland. I must stick to the facts. Once I saw the body, I'd know the truth. And if it was Ruby ... then I'd deal with it.

Although how I'd do that, I was uncertain.

Ten minutes later, I was in a chilly black police vehicle with Sergeant Matthers driving. Benji was squashed in beside me in the passenger seat as I clutched my handbag, staring straight ahead.

Given the late hour, the traffic was light, for which I was grateful. The mortuary was in Holgate, about a thirty-minute drive from the station.

Sergeant Matthers glanced at me. "Perhaps I should have contacted Jacob. He could meet us at the mortuary. He knows where it is."

"I sent him to Margate," I said. "And I'm not prepared to wait for him to return. We must deal with this swiftly."

"I'm sure it's not Ruby, but when I read the description, it worried me. I knew you'd want to know as soon as possible, just in case."

"You did the right thing," I said.

"When you told me you hadn't seen her for weeks, I thought it was strange. The two of you do everything together."

"Not so much recently," I said. "Work has kept me busy, and Ruby hasn't been well. She made light of it, but she seemed peaky. And she's off her beloved martinis! That's most unlike her."

"I'm no Jacob for solving crime, but I'll help you in any way I can," Sergeant Matthers said.

"You're an excellent fellow," I said. "And I'm glad to have you here."

He nodded, and we continued the rest of the journey in silence.

Sergeant Matthers pulled up outside a plain, brick-built building consisting of three floors. We sat in the car for a moment, staring at it.

"The mortuary only has one attendant in the evening," Sergeant Matthers said. "I telephoned ahead and told him we'd be visiting."

I could not look away from the building. What if Ruby was in there?

"I can go in on my own," Sergeant Matthers offered. "But if it is Ruby, we'll need an identification. A family member would also need to visit."

I drew in a steadying breath. "It won't come to that. There's no point in worrying Ruby's family until we know the truth."

We continued our silent vigil.

Benji rested a paw on my knee.

"You're quite right," I said to him. "Whatever's going on with Ruby won't be solved by us sitting here, too fearful to discover the truth."

"Whenever you're ready," Sergeant Matthers said gently.

I opened my door and climbed out, Benji following close behind.

Sergeant Matthers led the way to a set of double doors. He pressed the bell, and a moment later, a tall, thin-faced man with slicked-back hair opened the door. He wore a white medical coat and had a hangdog expression.

Sergeant Matthers signed us in at the desk, and we had to wait a moment while the attendant collected the keys.

"That's Albert," Sergeant Matthers muttered to me. "He's competent, but he doesn't say much. Reads a lot."

"A healthy appetite for literature always makes for an interesting mind."

"I'm never sure what's on his mind," Sergeant Matthers said. "He barely utters a word."

"Better a silent intellect than a chattering moron," I said.

Sergeant Matthers smiled faintly. "You're onto something there."

Albert led us down a long corridor to another set of double doors. He unlocked them. "The dog stays here."

I desperately wanted Benji with me but understood the logic.

Albert entered ahead of us, heading to a multi-tiered row of chilled containment units. "She's already out. Over here, under this cloth."

My heart stumbled into a cacophony of irregular beats as I followed. It won't be Ruby. It can't be Ruby.

"Are you ready?" Sergeant Matthers asked. "Albert will remove the covering so you can see the face."

I wasn't ready. I wanted to turn and run, but that was neither practical nor helpful. I nodded, unable to trust my voice.

Albert slowly lifted the cover, folding it to the woman's collarbone. I froze, needing a moment to steel myself before looking.

The hair was dark, just like Ruby's, but the skin was pallid and lifeless. No hint of Ruby's rosy glow. When my mind stopped its chaotic riot, I studied the woman's features. There was a startling similarity, but—thank heavens—it wasn't Ruby!

"It's not her. This woman is slightly older, and her nose is more upturned." I looked at Sergeant Matthers, torn between smiling and crying. The relief was overwhelming. "Do you know how she died?"

"She drowned," Albert said.

"You can cover her now," Sergeant Matthers said. Turning to me, he added, "We're unsure if it was an accident or suicide. She lacked identification, but the water may have washed it away. No one saw it happen. She was found on the Thames bank."

"Such a pity," I said. "She wasn't old. Are there any signs of a struggle?"

"There are no injuries on the body," Sergeant Matthers said. "It might have been a tragic accident. With any luck, someone will come forward to claim her."

"Let's hope so," I murmured.

After bidding Albert good night, I collected Benji and was relieved when we stepped out of the mortuary.

"After that shock, I'm calling it a night," I said. "Keep me updated about Inspector Finchley's plans for Dirk. And make sure he knows I'm not giving up. He'll feel like a fool when he realises Dirk is innocent."

"Of course. And I'll keep looking for Ruby, too," Sergeant Matthers said. "I'm sorry I put you through this."

"Don't give it another thought. I'm just glad someone else is searching for her, too."

Sergeant Matthers kindly dropped Benji and me home, and I was grateful to enter the house's safe, warm refuge.

"Veronica! Is that you? I was certain you'd abandoned us for good this time!" My mother's voice warbled out of her downstairs bedroom.

Shrugging off my coat, I felt a tightness in my shoulders. A murder and a missing friend were a lethal combination for rattling one's calm demeanour.

I headed into my mother's room with Benji, where she sat propped up in bed. Her glasses perched askew on her nose, and her fluffy grey hair suggested she hadn't left the bed all day. She'd probably spent it immersed in her books or napping.

Our two small foster puppies were snuggled against her, and Benji immediately nosed his way over to them.

I inspected the puppies. Each had a plump belly, and they happily slept.

"You haven't been working at the newspaper this late, have you?" my mother asked.

"Correct."

She tutted. "Which means you've been chasing after a murderer."

"Among other things." I rolled my stiff shoulders.

"You're taking on too much."

"I'm taking on just the right amount to keep my mind busy and my hands occupied."

"I kept a plate warm for you." Matthew wandered in, dressed in an oversized jumper and slouchy trousers. He handed me a warm plate of beef stew and two thick slices of homemade bread.

Only when my stomach growled did I realise how ravenous I was. "You're the perfect brother." I took the plate with a smile.

"There's food in the kitchen for Benji, too," Matthew said as he settled on the other side of my mother's bed, watching as I tucked into my food.

Benji shot off at the mention of food, abandoning his enthusiastic sniffing of the puppies.

"What's the latest on that dreadful business at the Jolly Cricketer?" My mother leaned forward, her curiosity palpable.

"They have a prime suspect. The wrong one," I said.

"I'm sure you told the police that," Matthew said.

"I had no choice. Inspector Finchley is being as stubborn as ever." I sighed then added, "This stew is delicious."

Matthew was a dab hand in the kitchen and responsible for most of our meals. We always ate well, thanks to him.

"Tell me everything," my mother said. "I despise gossip, but I have the neighbours coming over for afternoon tea tomorrow. I can't let them down by not knowing the latest!"

I stifled a yawn, the exhaustion from the evening catching up with me. "Tomorrow."

My mother pouted. "You're my only link to the outside world."

"Finish your dinner and then go to bed," Matthew said, giving her a stern look.

"Not yet! I must talk to Veronica about you know what!"

"It can wait until the morning," Matthew said. "Veronica can barely keep her eyes open."

"What business is this?" What scheme was my mother involving herself in this time?

"Business that can hold off until tomorrow," Matthew said.

My mother's expression softened as I stifled another yawn. "You're right. In the morning, we'll set the world to rights over crumpets."

Chapter 14

"Fetch the strawberry jam from the kitchen, Matthew," my mother said. "And freshen the teapot."

Matthew grumbled as he slid off the bed and slouched into the kitchen, his adorable dog, Felix, at his heel.

"You're perfectly capable of getting out of bed and fetching your own jam." I was in my usual spot at the end of Mother's large bed. Benji was beside me, and the puppies were snoozing while draped over my mother's feet.

"I've been having heart palpitations all night. Any exertion will push me over the edge. And I barely slept a wink!"

My mother looked more refreshed than I did. Although I'd been exhausted when I'd fallen into bed, my mind had churned with the previous day's events. The murder. Dirk's arrest. Ruby's vanishing act. Jacob's dubious evidence about what happened to my father.

"Are you coming down with something, too?" My mother peered at me over the top of her spectacles.

"Too? Who's ill?"

"Foolish girl! I'm always unwell. Even more so recently. I have a delicate constitution."

Matthew returned with a laden tray, including a pot of tea, jam, and a plate of warm crumpets. "You have the constitution of an ox. And the appetite of one."

"You cheeky thing." My mother helped herself to another crumpet.

"What's got you so concerned?" I asked, nodding thanks to Matthew as he poured me a cup of tea.

"I should put it out of my mind and not give it another thought," my mother said.

"What thoughts are you considering not having?"

"It's unbecoming. Entirely inappropriate." My mother bit into her jam-laden crumpet.

I looked at Matthew. "Will you help pull back this veil of vagueness?"

He smiled. "The gentleman Mother met in Margate wants to visit her in London."

"That's splendid news," I said. "I enjoyed Colonel Basil's company."

"It's wrong!" my mother said. "I can't have another man in this house."

"Then take him out for lunch."

"Out! I'm not leaving this house. I'm still recovering from our seaside visit," my mother said. "I should ignore his telephone calls. And the letters."

"I didn't realise there were letters, too." I arched an eyebrow.

My mother's cheeks flushed. "We're passing the time. We're both lonely and on our own. Our children have as good as abandoned us."

"We still live with you," Matthew pointed out.

My mother fed a small piece of crumpet to Benji, who sat obediently by the side of the bed, watching her every bite. "But you're both busy. Veronica with her career aspirations, and you lurking about in your bedroom, plotting who knows what."

"I mainly read or sleep," Matthew said. "You only have to call, and I'll come running."

"Even so, I always feel I'm on my own." My mother sniffed gently and leaned over to give Felix a piece of crumpet.

"That's even more reason to accept Colonel Basil's visit," I said. "If you're both lonely, you can keep each other company. There's no harm in it."

"I don't want the neighbours gossiping. You know how they love to gossip. It's despicable."

I failed not to chuckle. Mother adored gossip, even though she denied it.

"If that's what's worrying you, tell the neighbours he's a family friend," I said. "Not your special friend."

"Don't get ideas into your head," my mother said. "We're cordial with each other, but that's all. We grew friendly because we're of a similar age. Both of us have one foot in the grave."

"What do you think, Matthew?" I asked.

"I don't have enough experience to pass comment," he said. "Relationships cause trouble, though."

I winced. Matthew had had his heart ruthlessly broken by a rival journalist. I couldn't forgive Isabella for discarding my brother and never enjoyed it when our paths crossed.

"Enough about my troubles. I must know the latest on your murder investigation," my mother said.

"It's going in the wrong direction," I said. "The police are focusing on a journalist. Dirk Somerville. He'd had words with the victim and was writing a scandalous piece about him."

"Do you think Dirk's innocent?" Matthew asked.

"I'm certain of it. And I must visit the police station to speak to him. While there, I will bash sense into Inspector Finchley's hard head."

"Jacob should help you," my mother said. "He has his old contacts. Even though he almost got himself blown apart, the other officers respect him."

"Jacob is dealing with our Margate business," I said. "I'm planning to visit him this weekend. Although I'm not sure I'll have the time if this murder is still up in the air."

"He won't wait around forever," my mother said.

I sank my teeth into a warm, sweet crumpet. "I'm not sure I understand your meaning." My mother had been pressing for an engagement, followed by a swift marriage, ever since I told her Jacob and I were involved.

"Good men don't wait around. And there's a shortage since the war."

"Like butter," Matthew said.

"Jacob knows my character, and he's happy with it. We're both content."

My mother opened her mouth to continue debating with me, but Matthew stuck a crumpet in it.

I chortled as I finished my tea.

"Any news on Ruby?" Matthew asked.

"Nothing. Even Lady M is on the case."

"That girl is a menace to herself." My mother chomped on her extra crumpet. "But she's poor, so she can't be off anywhere fancy."

"She's not that poor!" Although her family had fallen on hard times and struggled to get out of the mess they'd made, Ruby earned a fair living through her work with Lady M.

"Has she got a new gentleman friend who's whisked her off somewhere exotic?" my mother asked.

"If she has, she's hiding him," I said. "I do hope she hasn't met someone unsuitable."

"She did enough of that when we were on holiday," my mother said. "Although that French chap was delicious to look at."

"He was Italian. He was a cad. There was nothing good about him," I said. "Now, I really must get to work."

"Wait! I need more information," my mother said. "What about other suspects in the murder investigation?"

"You've got enough out of me for now. It will keep the neighbours happy." I stood. "Thank you for breakfast, Matthew."

He nodded as I left the bedroom with my mother still complaining, Benji by my side. It was time to focus on the dead.

I spent the rest of my day making telephone calls and writing obituaries. The tale of a farmer who'd spent his life being unkind to the pigs he was supposed to care for had intrigued me. Apparently, late one evening, he'd had too much to drink and stumbled into a pen. The pigs enacted a fitting revenge. There'd been barely anything left of the chap, except his glass eye and a few bones.

His widow described him as 'a mean drunk who got what he deserved,' but she asked me not to quote her on that.

"Veronica, have you got a minute?" Uncle Harry poked his head out of his office and gestured for me to come in.

I grabbed my notepad and headed into the office with Benji.

"I hear the police have their man for Sir Gerald Langton's murder." Uncle Harry gestured to a seat.

"They've got a man, but it's the wrong one," I said as I settled on the chair.

"I recognise the suspect's name. Dirk Somerville. He's a journalist?"

"That's right. I know him, too. According to Sergeant Matthers, Dirk was investigating a possible financial scandal that involved Sir Gerald."

"Interesting. I know a few people in banking and investments. I'll see what I can find out."

Uncle Harry had an endless list of contacts. He'd worked in journalism most of his life and had a personality everyone warmed to. People opened up to him and told him their deepest, darkest secrets, which was a terrible idea when speaking to a journalist.

I waited patiently in the chair, stroking Benji and looking around my uncle's cluttered office as he worked his magic. He asked a few questions but listened far more than he talked. It was a key journalistic skill.

"Thanks, Clifford. I owe you a pint for that," Uncle Harry said, finishing his telephone call and placing the receiver back in its cradle. "There's truth in the financial scandal."

"What was Sir Gerald involved in?" I asked.

"He had a reputation for making big promises and not delivering. He'd take people's money, say they were onto a sure thing with a stock market investment, but it never materialised."

"Was it deliberate fraud or poor financial management?"

"From what I've gleaned, Sir Gerald knew what he was doing. He had dozens of unhappy clients. Of course, he blamed a poor-performing stock market and claimed he'd warned them about the risks."

"While saying he'd double their money, I suppose?" I shook my head. "Dirk must have uncovered some iron-clad information and planned to publish."

Uncle Harry leaned back in his seat, his brow furrowed. "If Dirk was writing this story, he wouldn't ruin it by killing Sir Gerald. A dead man will always garner sympathy."

"That's what I said to Inspector Finchley. Dirk gains nothing from this murder."

"Kill the crucial lead in the story, and you have no story," Uncle Harry said.

"Which means the police are focused on the wrong man," I said. "I know it wasn't Dirk. He's a solid character."

"I don't know his work well. Isn't his focus sports?"

"That's why he was at the charity cricket event," I said. "Now we know he was investigating Sir Gerald, so perhaps he had ulterior motives for attending."

"Do you intend to prove the police wrong?" Uncle Harry asked.

"Only if they continue along the incorrect path," I said. "There are other credible leads."

Uncle Harry stood, walked around his desk, and shut the door before returning to his seat. "Don't you think you've got enough on your plate?"

"People keep saying that, but I have a rather large plate. And you know I like to keep busy."

Uncle Harry fixed me with a knowing look, remaining silent for several seconds. "Jacob's been asking questions about your father. Did you know about that?"

I jerked in my seat. "How did you find out?"

He spread his hands. "It's what I do. I keep my finger on the pulse. And when the news touches a family member, I pay close attention."

I let out a long breath. "Jacob's been following leads. He thinks someone had a hand in my father's death."

"Veronica!" Uncle Harry's voice sharpened. "We know what happened to him."

"We thought we did. But I never understood why ... why he did it. Dad had a good life. He loved his work, even when it kept him so busy. That's how he was. Always chasing the next idea, the next investment. He was unstoppable."

"And you take after him," Uncle Harry said. "You rarely sit still for five minutes."

"I've been at my desk all day, crafting obituaries."

"You know what I mean." Uncle Harry's tone softened. "You've always got a dozen things rattling around in that head of yours." He leaned forward. "Don't dwell on the past. It'll bring heartache. Davey is gone."

"I know," I mumbled. "But wouldn't you want to know if it was murder? If it was, wouldn't you want justice?"

Uncle Harry's gaze grew intense. "Who wanted him dead? Jacob is wasting his time, and yours, by chasing shadows and giving you false hope."

"I'm glad Jacob told me his concerns," I said. "But for all his prodding, it's come to nothing. I've asked Jacob not to keep looking into it. Even so..."

"You can't get it out of your thoughts?"

"Now the question is out there, I don't want to let it go."

"You should." Uncle Harry's voice carried the weight of years of wisdom. "Dragging up this business won't bring anyone happiness. And if you uncover a dark truth about how your father died, how will that help you?"

My hands were clenched in my lap. "You know what I'd do."

"That's what worries me." Uncle Harry let out a weary sigh. "You have a fabulous life. A life many people dream of but never achieve. Are you willing to risk all of that for vengeance?"

"Wouldn't you if Jacob discovered someone killed my father? Your brother!"

"I'd think about it, yes," Uncle Harry admitted. "But I'd also think about what Davey would have wanted. Do you think he'd encourage you to throw your life away?"

I blinked away the haze in my eyes. "No. He wouldn't."

"Then focus on the good you have. Plan for the future. And tell Jacob to give this up. Spend your time together looking forward. That is, if you see a future with him."

I hesitated then nodded. I did. Jacob hadn't shared this information with me to stir trouble. He knew I valued the truth. Jacob was a good man. An honest man.

Uncle Harry smiled. "Why don't you head off early? Make some time for Jacob now?"

"There's no point. He's in Margate," I said.

"Telephone him and ask him to come back," Uncle Harry said. "I've seen how hard you've been working. Jacob can catch a train, and you can meet him at the station. Go to a show and have dinner together. Plan fun, rather than always looking into the darkness."

"That all sounds extravagant!"

Uncle Harry pulled out his wallet and handed me a few notes. "As your uncle and your employer, I insist. A stressed employee makes for a poor journalist."

I jumped up and kissed him on the cheek.

"That's quite enough of that." Uncle Harry briefly squeezed my hand after he'd tucked the notes into my palm. "I just want to see you happy."

"I am. Thank you." I returned to my desk and telephoned Jacob in our Margate office, ignoring Bob's withering stare when he realised I was making a personal call.

"Vale Detective Agency," Jacob answered briskly. "Jacob Templeton speaking."

"Are we sticking with that name?" I asked. "Perhaps it should be Vale and Templeton Detective Agency."

"Templeton and Vale sounds better," he replied, his voice full of mock seriousness. "Only because we're going alphabetically."

I chuckled. "Naturally. Anyway, I've got good news. I've been given the rest of the afternoon off. Would you be able to get back here for an evening meal? Uncle Harry's treating us to dinner and a show."

"Do we have something to celebrate?"

"No, but I've been working too hard and neglecting you. What do you say?"

"That sounds perfect. Although I don't feel neglected."

"Well, then, consider this a treat. But don't get used to it."

Jacob paused. "I was thinking of coming back early, anyway."

"You're missing me that much?"

He didn't laugh. "I always miss you. But … I received something in the post. Something you need to see."

Chapter 15

I paced the main concourse of Victoria train station, no Benji by my side since theatres and fine dining restaurants weren't hospitable to dogs.

The train rumbled into the station. I stepped out of the way as passengers disembarked. It was a full train, returning people home after work, so I had to wait several minutes before spotting Jacob. His walk was brisk, even with his slight limp. The tension in his face eased when he saw me, and he smiled.

"You're right on time." I pressed a kiss to his cheek.

"The service from Kent is always reliable," Jacob said.

I stepped back, glancing at his briefcase.

"Not here," he said. "I thought we were being treated to dinner and a show?"

"I won't be able to wait that long," I said.

"Let's get settled before we talk." Jacob held out his crooked elbow for me to take. "Have you purchased tickets yet?"

"No. I thought we'd try our luck on the door. You can get a bargain if you wait until the last minute."

He arched an eyebrow. "A sold-out show means we could find ourselves wandering the streets of London."

"If we can't get in, we'll find another theatre," I said. "Theatrical productions are more Ruby's thing than mine, anyway. I only go with her because they make her happy."

"Let's start with dinner and see how things go," Jacob suggested.

"Things?"

"Exactly. After our discussion."

His tone made me uneasy, but I remained silent as we left the train station and headed towards the restaurant. I'd booked an early dining slot, so we'd have plenty of time for the theatre afterwards.

It was a small restaurant, intimately lit, with only a dozen tables. I preferred a more private dining experience than a rowdy rabble of diners to distract from one's companion.

"I'm sorry. Your table's not ready yet," the waiter said apologetically. "We had a birthday party this afternoon, and they over-stayed. It won't be long. Please accept a complimentary drink at the bar while you wait."

We settled ourselves on high bar stools. Jacob ordered half a pint of ale, and I opted for a gin fizz.

"Will you ever reveal your secret to me?" I asked, after taking a long sip of my drink. "You said I needed to see something, but you haven't shown it to me yet. I don't even know what this is about."

Jacob lifted his briefcase onto his lap and snapped the locks open. "I'm hesitating because I don't know what to make of the information."

"Is it a fresh case? The fraud matter?"

"It's about a case, but an old one." Jacob flipped open the lid of his briefcase. "As you know, I've been looking into the rumours surrounding your father's death."

"I thought that business was over. You came to a dead end. The people claiming to have information were trying to extort money." I shook my head. "I despise people who prey on others' weaknesses."

"Which is why I ended communication and stopped pursuing that lead. But then I received these photographs in the post." Jacob passed me a small brown envelope.

The address of our new office in Margate was neatly printed on it, but there was no stamp, meaning someone had hand-delivered it.

I set down my drink and tipped out the contents of the envelope. There were three black-and-white photographs inside.

"Take a minute and study them," Jacob said. "Then let me know what you think. I can't quite believe it myself."

I spread the photographs along the bar. They showed a group of men who looked like they were out for an afternoon of fun. They wore casual clothing, with shirtsleeves rolled up and collars open. The venue was outside. Coastal. It looked warm.

I studied the men's faces. One caught my eye. I inhaled sharply and peered closer at the photograph.

"It's him, isn't it?" Jacob asked.

"When were these taken?"

"There was a brief note included with the photographs," Jacob said. "The person who sent them claims they were taken within the last six months."

I lifted the photograph that had the clearest image. "This man bears a shocking likeness to my father."

"The photographs look recent," Jacob said.

I turned the photograph over. Since the back was unprinted, I couldn't determine their location or production date. "These can't be legitimate. I agree that might be my father, but the photographs date and location are indeterminable."

"Look again."

I studied the image some more. Something wasn't right. The more I looked at the photograph, the more I realised it could be no one else but my father. But he looked older! Older than the last time I'd seen him alive.

That was impossible. This must be a man who looked eerily like him. If I met this chap in the street, I'd do a double take, convinced it was my dead father.

"Can you see now why I didn't want to discuss this over the telephone?" Jacob asked.

"Whoever gave these to you has a most unpleasant sense of humour," I said. "I suppose there was a request for money for the rest of the information? The proof of where and when the photographs were taken? Much like the case I'm investigating, promises were made but never delivered upon. It will be the same here."

"Surprisingly, they sent no request for money," Jacob said.

"There'll be a demand for funds," I said. "This has to be someone's vile attempt at cheating us. They know you've been asking about my father, and they've figured out a way to exploit us. Or so they think. More fool them."

"I've been discreet."

"Not discreet enough. Uncle Harry got wind of what you're doing. He said it would cause trouble, and here we are!"

"It's hard to keep anything from your Uncle Harry," Jacob said. "When I worked for the police, he knew the information almost before we did. He certainly had an inside source or two on his payroll."

"I have no doubt he does," I said. "It's how he gets the best stories."

Jacob sat back, sipping his ale and giving me time to think.

"What do you want to do?" he asked after several minutes had passed.

"Nothing! Without context as to when, where, and who took these photographs, they're useless."

"He looks older, don't you think?"

"Yes! Which is why it can't possibly be him." I found it hard to tear my gaze from the images. I longed for it to be my father, but it was impossible.

"When I was talking to people, there was caginess when speaking about your father," Jacob said.

I set down the photograph and gave him my full attention. "I won't deny he had a reputation. He could be ruthless when chasing a business he wanted to purchase."

"I heard mention of how determined he was when he set his sights on something," Jacob said. "But it wasn't just that."

"What are you suggesting?" The direction of this conversation led to an icy ball of concern lodging in the pit of my stomach.

"Veronica, your father was of interest to the police for years. We never found proof, but we know he obtained a sizeable chunk of his initial investments through less-than-legitimate means. No bank would lend him money, so he found it elsewhere."

I shuffled the photographs into a neat pile and tucked them back into the envelope. "That was before my time. Besides, if he gathered funds from inappropriate sources, and I'm not saying he did, he'd have paid it back. He was a legitimate businessman."

"And you're an astute woman. You've heard the rumours about his connections to criminal gangs to fund his empire."

"Empire! He bought rundown pubs and renovated them."

"But where did his money come from?" Jacob asked. "How did he get started?"

A rattle of anger shuddered through me. "He wasn't a saint. And he rubbed shoulders with a few individuals he shouldn't have. But my father never broke the law. And I regularly inspect the pub books, so I know there's nothing dubious about them. I run a clean business."

"I'm not saying you don't. But what if your father found himself in trouble with the people he borrowed money from?"

"If there had been trouble, it would have happened many years ago," I said.

"Or he hid things from the family because he didn't want to worry you."

"No! I refuse to believe that," I said. "Besides, he trained me to take over this business. He would never have done that if he knew trouble would come my way. My father was insistent on keeping the family safe."

"Which is why he concealed this information from you," Jacob said.

"What was he concealing?" I asked.

"The information that got him killed."

"Not killed. Dead!" My breath was ragged and kept sticking in my throat.

"What if the photograph proves he isn't?"

I jerked back in my seat. "That is too shocking to consider. If that is him, and this photograph was taken in the last six months, that means..."

"He abandoned his family," Jacob said.

"But he died," I whispered. "We found his things abandoned on Beachy Head."

Jacob rested a hand on top of mine. "Most people who choose that way out leave a note. There was no note with your father's things. I've been reviewing his old case records over and over."

"It could have blown away. And he wasn't in his right mind when he did such a thing," I said. "No person ever is. How do you expect him to write a note explaining things when he was in such a terrible predicament?"

"Or your father didn't leave a note because he didn't die," Jacob said. "He staged the scene because he needed to vanish."

I looked away, blinking back tears of shock and surprise.

"At first, when I reviewed his case, it made me pause," Jacob said. "As you told me, your father had everything. There was no reason he'd want to die."

I dislodged the lump in my throat by downing most of my gin fizz. "I need time to think. He was a family man. He adored us."

"Perhaps he saw this as the safest way out. If everybody assumed he was dead, they'd stop looking for him or trying to punish him by hurting his family."

"Who?" I demanded. "Who was looking for him?"

"I can't know for certain, but I sense it's connected to how he first came into his money," Jacob said.

"I'll ask my mother," I said. "She'll know. They went into the venture together."

"Is it wise to worry her?"

"I'll ... I'll say I'm curious about how the business got started. And there are records. I can look through the old files. That will prove you're wrong."

Jacob exhaled slowly. "I hope you can. I don't want you to be angry with me, but I couldn't leave you in the dark. Even if there's an outside possibility the man in the photograph is your father, and that man is still alive, you have a right to know."

My breath came out shaky as I struggled to gather my thoughts. Could this be true? Could my father be alive? Had something gone so wrong in the business that he'd chosen to abandon us rather than face it together? That didn't sound like my father at all.

"Keep looking into it," I finally said. "And find the source of these photographs. Then we'll figure out our next step."

"What a step it'll be," Jacob said.

I jabbed a finger against the envelope. "Until I see him in the flesh, I won't believe these photographs. And until then, all I want to do is focus on murder. Sir Gerald's.

That, at least, I can influence." I pushed the photographs back towards Jacob, who slid them into his briefcase.

"If you want to talk about your father more—"

"I don't," I interrupted. "I'm focused on Inspector Finchley's continued incompetence. He still has my friend Dirk as his prime suspect. Although, after Dirk's foolish escape attempt, I understand why the police are interested in him."

Jacob regarded me thoughtfully then nodded, realising, most sensibly, I wouldn't relent. "Who do you favour as Sir Gerald's killer?"

My rattled emotions settled into place as I shifted my focus. "There's Eleanor. Sir Gerald's mistress. She had motive but little opportunity."

"She must have learned to be discreet, given she was carrying on behind her husband's back," Jacob said. "Perhaps she saw a chance to slip away to the cellar."

"That's possible. Then there's her sister, Finella. She had an opportunity, but I see no motive. Sir Gerald was a stranger to her."

"Was he such a stranger?" Jacob mused. "It might be sensible to speak to her again. She could have concealed her sister's affair to protect her reputation."

"True enough," I said. "We also have Reginald Harcourt. A motive, but what about his opportunity?"

"Eleanor's husband strikes me as a logical candidate," Jacob said.

"Charles Pembroke has a prime motive, and there's a small window of opportunity. I favour him as well. Although Inspector Finchley thinks he's splendid and a pillar of the local business community."

"Someone's lying to you." Jacob's gaze flicked to the briefcase. "It would appear more than one person hasn't been truthful with you."

I scowled at the closed briefcase, the photographs still jangling my sensibilities. "The least said about that, the better. For the rest of the evening, I'd appreciate it if we could only talk about who clubbed Sir Gerald to death and then dared to dump his body in my cellar."

A polite throat-clearing behind me drew my attention. I turned to see a startled waiter.

"Your ... your table is ready," he said.

Jacob chuckled as he finished his drink. "You're already intimidating the staff, and we haven't even had our first course."

Chapter 16

My mother regarded my barely touched bowl of porridge. "Are you ailing?"

"No, I leave the ailing to you."

She tutted. "Then whatever is wrong?"

"I have a lot on my mind," I said.

"When most women go out for dinner and then to the theatre with their gentleman friend, they're all smiles and full of happy tales. Don't tell me you and Jacob argued?"

"We often argue. We enjoy the sport," I said.

My mother sighed. "You'll never keep a man if you're prickly towards him."

"Jacob likes my prickle. Let's leave that topic of conversation be, shall we?"

The petulant tut that escaped my mother's lips suggested she planned on doing the opposite.

"Matthew! Talk sense into your sister. All this glumness won't do. She won't make a happy marital home if she mopes over her food and refuses to speak."

Matthew set down a tray of smashed-up raw mince and a small bowl of milk. "I'm not getting involved. The puppies need feeding."

"Not on the bed! The last time you fed them, they got so excited they had an accident on my favourite blanket." Mother clutched her sheets.

Matthew scooped up the puppies and placed them on the floor before sitting next to them, gently pushing away their eager noses as they sniffed at their breakfast.

Benji and Felix sat at a respectable distance, although their ears were pricked, waiting to clear the leftovers.

"If you don't have a mind for porridge, Matthew will make you toast," my mother said to me.

"Matthew literally has his hands full," I replied. "And if I desire toast, I'll make it myself."

My mother lifted her hands and dropped them onto her bedcovers. "Is it Ruby? You girls are close, so I assume you share everything. But now she's gallivanting with her mysterious fancy man, you have no one to speak to. It's not healthy."

"We don't know Ruby is gallivanting anywhere," I said. "Although Sergeant Matthers is helping me look for her."

My mother gasped. "She's got herself in dreadful trouble, hasn't she? It must be that if the police are involved."

I nudged away the unpleasant memories of my visit to the mortuary. "Ruby is healthy and hearty and off having a fine old time. I just wish she'd drop me a note to say what she's doing."

"She must have desired a break from all the snooping around and getting herself into trouble while you try to do police business," my mother said.

"Veronica does do police business." Matthew had one puppy tucked between his knees and the other under one arm, using his free hand to scoop in mouthfuls of mince, which they greedily devoured. "And with her private detective agency in full swing, she'll make even more of a name for herself."

"I don't agree with it. It's such dangerous work," my mother said. "Although it will give you the inside scoop on the latest criminal activities."

"I'm happy to share news of Jacob's financial fraud case," I said. "But it's based down in Kent, so it won't interest the neighbours when you gather for a gossip over tea and cake."

My mother waved a hand in the air, dismissing my words. "I need local news! That's what fascinates us. We need to be prepared. With danger lurking around every corner, we must know what we're about to face."

"This is a safe street. And our nosy neighbours, you included, will report any stranger wandering about and send them away with a flea in their ear."

"I'm not nosy! I'm curious."

"Veronica takes after you," Matthew said. "It's why she's so well suited to her career choices."

I shot him a grateful smile. Most days, I could accommodate my mother's persistent questioning and fretting, but after last night's shocking conversation with Jacob, my thoughts refused to settle. Our dinner had been pleasant, but we'd abandoned the idea of the theatre and taken a long walk instead.

All the while, the photograph that showed the man who looked like my father kept presenting itself. I couldn't believe he was alive. If he was, he'd be in our lives. None of it made any sense, and when I came across a puzzle I couldn't unravel, it displeased me.

"There you go again with that wistful look in your eyes," my mother said.

"I need to get to work," I said.

"Murder business or dead person business?" Matthew asked.

"Uncle Harry let me have time off yesterday," I said, "so I'll have obituaries to catch up on."

"Give me a minute to finish here, and I'll walk you out," Matthew said.

That was unlike Matthew. He must need to talk to me about something.

I helped him with the squirming puppies and then gave the leftovers to Benji and Felix. We headed into the kitchen to wash up and take the puppies outside to do their business.

I glanced at Matthew. He stood on the doorstep, his hands in his pockets as he rocked back and forth. "Out with it. What do you want to tell me you didn't want Mother to overhear?"

He grinned at me. "I can't keep anything from you, can I?"

"You've never been able to keep secrets," I said. "And when you have something to hide, that's what you actually do. We don't see you for days."

He grimaced. "I've been better recently. Having Felix helps. I've taken him out every day. Sometimes I only get to the end of the road and have to turn back, but I'm improving."

I reached over and squeezed his arm. "I'm happy to hear it. Dogs should be on the doctor's prescription pad. They're nature's cure for all worries. I always feel happier when I have Benji with me."

"I'm glad I kept Felix," Matthew said.

"Is that what you're worried about? Felix isn't sick, is he? We can take him to the very best vets. Money is no object."

"No, there are no problems there. Felix is in fine form. I'm worried about Mother, though."

"A new health problem?"

"No, the old ones occupy her attention." Matthew shook his head good-naturedly and rolled his eyes. "But I overheard her conversation with Colonel Basil last night. He's been calling every evening. He's persistent."

"I don't see that as a problem," I said. "He's a healthy distraction. Mother gets lonely stuck in this house, even though being stuck is of her own making."

"I thought the same too, but she was telling him all about the house and how big it is. He must have been asking questions. It got me thinking..."

"Go on."

"Maybe Colonel Basil isn't interested in her but her assets?"

"You're suggesting he's after her money?"

"Our family isn't poor," Matthew said. "We don't flash money around, but you're always well turned out, even if you're covered in dog fur. And when Mother forces me to the bakery, she insists on the best cakes. I tell her I can make her something, but she only wants the most expensive. And then there's the silverware and fancy crockery that never gets used. And the business income. I know that's your concern, but I'm sure the pubs do well."

I exhaled slowly. "Perhaps we should look closer into Colonel Basil's background. He may think the family is an easy target. I'd never have considered it. When we met, he appeared well-to-do."

"I thought the same. What if it was an act?" Matthew checked over his shoulder. "And Mother can be difficult. She's not everybody's cup of tea."

"I remember when she was full of life and laughter," I said. "Our parents were happy together. She complained when he travelled for work, but they were always so joyful to be reunited. I thought the fact they had separate lives added something extra to their marriage. They never took each other for granted."

"You've got a point. Of course, that changed after Father died."

I bit my tongue, briefly considering sharing the photograph news with Matthew, but false hope was a terrible thing.

"They devoted themselves to each other," I said. "And I saw flickers of who Mother used to be when she was with Colonel Basil."

Matthew rubbed the back of his neck. "I don't want to interfere, not if he's making her happy. But it has me concerned."

"We'll monitor the situation," I said. "Perhaps all he wants is happiness, just like the rest of us. He saw beneath Mother's fretting and worrying about her health and spotted her true character."

"I hope so," Matthew said. "Let's get these puppies inside before they wiggle out under the fence and we have to chase them through the traffic."

Having scooped up the puppies, cleaned them of mud and breakfast leftovers, and settled them on my mother's bed, I gathered my things to go to work.

The telephone in the hallway stopped me in my tracks. I picked it up and discovered Sergeant Matthers on the other end of the line.

"I'm glad I caught you," he said. "I've got bad news, and I knew you'd want to hear it as soon as possible."

"Is it about the case?" I asked.

"Inspector Finchley intends to charge Dirk with Sir Gerald's murder."

I gritted my teeth. "Inspector Finchley is a moron."

There was a strangled laugh from Sergeant Matthers. "I wouldn't say that, but Detective Chief Inspector Taylor yelled at him first thing this morning. There's been pressure from all sides to get this matter resolved sharpish. And Dirk's alibi is non-existent. We've done some digging and can't find anyone who saw him walking to his lodgings on the afternoon of the murder."

"That doesn't make him guilty, just unlucky."

"What's to say he didn't sneak back to the charity event? He got Sir Gerald into the cellar and set about him. That's the story Inspector Finchley is telling, anyway."

"What about Dirk's wooden leg?" I asked. "Is there evidence that ties it to the crime?"

"We're still waiting on the test results," Sergeant Matthers said. "We hope to have them through by the end of the day."

"And in the meantime, you confine Dirk to a cell where he must hop around one-legged, panicking that he's about to be charged with a murder he didn't commit. It's grossly unfair."

"He's comfortable. I'm making sure of that," Sergeant Matthers said. "And I've told him we're looking into things together, outside of the official investigation."

"You're an excellent chap," I said. "But we must hurry. If Inspector Finchley plans to charge him today, we have no time to waste. Do you know where Dirk lives?"

"I do. Why do you ask?"

I checked the time. I'd be late getting to work, but this matter wouldn't wait. "Give me the details, and I'll meet you there. We have an investigation to conduct."

After waiting for Sergeant Matthers to provide me with the address, we said our goodbyes, and I hung up.

"Who was that?" Mother called from her bed.

"Just a bit of business," I said. "I'll see you this evening."

"Wait! Is it about the murder? I must know everything."

"Later, I promise." I raced out through the front door with Benji, hailed a taxi since my car was still being repaired, and shot across London to the rundown area of Wandsworth. It was best known for its grim prison, and I feared, if things didn't go Dirk's way, that was where he'd end up.

When I arrived, Sergeant Matthers was waiting outside a large shabby property that had seen better days.

He nodded at me. "I've already alerted the landlord we need a word. I found him emptying Dirk's room."

"I hope you told him to stop," I said. "There could be vital evidence in there."

"He wasn't happy, but I sent him off for a mug of tea and a cigarette while we take another look."

"Then we'd better get to work," I said.

Sergeant Matthers pushed open the front door and led me along a damp-smelling hallway with sticky carpeting underfoot to the furthest room on the left.

It was a dingy affair. The wallpaper was a faded brownish-yellow. A single bed sat against one wall, with a pile of clothing heaped on the floor. There was no wardrobe to hang things in. The room had an air of sadness and neglect. But one corner stood out from the rest.

A large wooden desk dominated the room. It was old, and the surface was scratched and marked. The desk was vast, covered in carefully stacked piles of paper. It wasn't messy. There was a method to Dirk's filing.

I headed to the desk while Benji sniffed around.

"That's where we found the information about the stories Dirk's been working on." Sergeant Matthers joined me. "Most of the notes are sports-related. There were also scribblings on the charity cricket event and a couple of scandal pieces about socialites. Nothing significant. No one from the cricket event. And then we discovered this."

He handed me a set of papers. It was Dirk's research on Sir Gerald's business activities.

"At first, I couldn't make head nor tail of it, but as we read through the documents, it became clear. Sir Gerald has been investing other people's money into a fake scheme."

I read through the information at triple speed. "My word! Not just that. He's been pulling others into it, getting them to sell the scheme to their friends. They get a cut of the investment, while the investors get nothing but disappointment."

"That's the size of it."

"Surely Sir Gerald realised he couldn't get away with that forever."

"He was clever," Sergeant Matthers replied. "Although he sold the scheme as a guaranteed win, when you read the small print, it describes the investment as high risk. There's no guarantee of any profit. How many people read the small print of anything?"

"I always do," I said.

"Good for you," Sergeant Matthers said with a faint smile. "Sir Gerald relied on his good name, wealth, and connections. If a friend asked you to invest in a surefire thing, why would you question it? You don't expect your friends to do you wrong. That's how he was getting away with it."

"He must have had an escape plan," I said. "This ruse would have come back to haunt him when he got the wrong wealthy individual involved, and they brought the full force of the law down on his head. It would have been the end of him."

"Sir Gerald owned properties abroad," Sergeant Matthers said. "Some of those countries don't have extradition treaties with Britain. When the game was up, he could have fled and started a new life using everyone else's money."

"What a dreadful business," I said, shaking my head. "Shouldn't you be able to rely on your friends?"

"Just like you do with Miss Ruby," Sergeant Matthers said. "I keep thinking about her. Any news?"

I carefully leafed through the paperwork on Dirk's desk. "I'm keeping my chin up and hoping for the best. But I'll be having strong words with her when she resurfaces. Her disappearance is inconsiderate."

"If it's any consolation, I've heard nothing to make you worry about her."

"No more bodies?"

"Always. But unless Ruby has gained fifty pounds and grown a grey beard, it's not her."

I smiled ruefully. "I appreciate you keeping an eye on the situation."

Sergeant Matthers pulled a crumpled brown bag from his pocket and offered me a peppermint. "She'll have some tale to tell when she shows her face."

"Of that, I have no doubt." I paused as I examined a sheet of paper on Dirk's desk. It was a list of names, most of them heavily crossed through and unreadable. "Have you looked at this?"

"We checked everything."

"This must be a list of Sir Gerald's contacts. I recognise most of the names. All influential chaps, mostly from the world of finance. I can't make them all out, though."

"Inspector Finchley saw the list," Sergeant Matthers said. "He couldn't read it. Sir Gerald must have been thinking about who he could involve in this scheme as either an investor or to work for him."

"Have you spoken to these people?" I asked.

"The ones we could identify," Sergeant Matthers replied. "We asked Dirk about the list and where he got it from. He said it was part of his research. He's been in contact with some of them, too, although most wouldn't talk to him. Dirk said they sounded embarrassed or worried. They didn't want to look foolish."

"I'm sure they don't," I said. "Especially if Sir Gerald fleeced them out of their money."

I lifted the sheet of paper and held it up to the window. One name caught my eye. It began with the letters REG. "Could this be Reginald Harcourt?"

Sergeant Matthers peered over my shoulder. "I can't say for certain, but it looks like an 'H' at the beginning of the surname."

"If Sir Gerald cheated money out of Reginald," I said, "that could change everything."

Sergeant Matthers grimaced.

I patted his arm. "Would you like me to break the news to our dear inspector that he's missed a vital clue?"

He sighed. "No. I'll never enjoy being yelled at, but I'd better tell him."

Chapter 17

"We already have our man for Sir Gerald's murder!" Inspector Finchley slapped down the papers I'd brought to the police station from Dirk's lodgings. "You had no right to snoop around evidence when the police have done a thorough job. And you!" He jabbed a finger at Sergeant Matthers. "Are you looking to be demoted? Or sacked?"

"No, sir!"

I glanced at Sergeant Matthers, who bravely stood behind me as Inspector Finchley unleashed his fury upon us. Benji stood beside Sergeant Matthers to give him some much-needed comfort.

"The list of scribbled-out names is vitally important," I said. "They're people Sir Gerald was recruiting to his fake investment scheme or planning to steal from. Reginald Harcourt is on that list!"

"I checked that list myself. Most of the names were unreadable."

"My eyesight is better than yours. And Sergeant Matthers agrees with me."

Inspector Finchley glowered at poor Sergeant Matthers.

"Reginald attended the charity cricket event, and he left during our luncheon," I said.

"We know why he left the event," Inspector Finchley said. "And we've been to his house. His maid confirmed she saw him. He couldn't have been in the cellar of the Jolly Cricketer and his house at the same time."

That was a setback. If Reginald had a cast-iron alibi, he couldn't have killed Sir Gerald.

"You should still let Dirk go," I said. "You've got no firm evidence to hold him."

"The tests on the murder weapon will be back any time now," Inspector Finchley said.

"It's a dreadful business. You shouldn't have taken Dirk's false leg," I said. "How is he supposed to walk?"

"We've provided him with a cane! He can get around fine."

"We were planning on speaking to Dirk again," Sergeant Matthers said.

"Yes! We've got him on the ropes," Inspector Finchley said. "If we can get a confession, we'll close the case by the end of the day."

"A confession from an innocent man won't be easy to achieve," I replied.

Sergeant Matthers shuffled his feet. "Dirk requested the interview. He wants to come clean about the story he was writing. He said it was important."

"Since I'm here, I'd appreciate sitting in," I said.

"Have you learned to hold your tongue?" Inspector Finchley asked

"Sadly not. Although I'm very speedy on the telephone," I said with a faint smile. "It's important to keep Lady M up to date on this matter, since this investigation greatly interests her."

Inspector Finchley sighed heavily and glared at Sergeant Matthers again. "Let's get this over with."

A few minutes later, we settled into our respective seats. Once again, I had a chair in the corner with Benji sitting beside me. Inspector Finchley and Sergeant Matthers sat on the opposite side of Dirk at a small table.

Even though he looked exhausted and dishevelled, he smiled warmly at me. "I'm glad to hear you're still fighting my corner."

"Until the bitter end." I gestured Benji over to Dirk. "I know you didn't do this."

"That's enough of that," Inspector Finchley snapped. "Dirk, you claim to have vital information regarding the story you were writing about Sir Gerald. We've read your notes, so I doubt you have anything to add. If this is a stalling tactic, we won't look kindly upon you when sentencing is due."

Dirk twisted in his seat and gave Inspector Finchley his full attention, one hand on Benji's head as he rested his chin on Dirk's knee. "I didn't want to say anything before, because this is an exclusive story. If I can get this out before anyone else, it'll be the making of me. I'll have my pick of newspapers to work for. Make a name for myself."

"It's not worth holding back if it will save you from prison," I said.

Dirk ran a hand over his stubbled chin. "I know. But I've been working on this for a long time. I was so close. Then Sir Gerald is murdered!"

"Because you realised there was more opportunity to get your pick of work by reporting a murder. You killed Sir Gerald and made yourself the exclusive reporter on-site," Inspector Finchley said. "But it didn't go according to plan, did it?"

I tutted at how ridiculous that possibility was, earning a glare from Inspector Finchley.

Dirk sighed. "There's no point in keeping secrets if I spend the rest of my life behind bars. And I can see that's where this is heading. So, here's the truth. Sir Gerald and Reginald were running a money scam together."

I inhaled sharply. "Reginald knew about the con?"

Dirk nodded. "But there was a problem. Reginald had invested in another of Sir Gerald's schemes. He got scared. When he learned the ins and outs of Sir Gerald's financial deception, he thought he was being conned, too. He demanded his money back, but Sir Gerald refused."

"I can't imagine a man of Reginald Harcourt's standing is used to being told no," I said.

Inspector Finchley raised his eyebrows and glared at me. "Why would Reginald give Sir Gerald money if he knew he was financially dishonest?"

"The investment happened before Sir Gerald's current scheme was in place," Dirk explained. "They've known each other for years, and Sir Gerald had a reputation for being an astute businessman. Of course, he had losses, but he always said, your failings are learning experiences. If you've never faced troubled times, you won't know how to deal with them when the next one comes along. He had a way with words."

"Did you ever interview Sir Gerald when gathering information for your story?" I asked.

"Once. But I never got beneath the polished surface of respectability," Dirk said. "I pretended I wanted to feature him as a prominent London businessman. He peacocked during the interview, flattered by my words, but whenever I probed about investment strategies, he'd shut me down. He must have realised I was investigating something suspicious because his office refused my next interview request."

"That rebuttal must have got your attention," I said.

"It did. Sir Gerald was a proud man with a big ego. Of course, he'd want to be featured in a newspaper article showcasing his brilliance. It would bring more willing victims to his door and make him wealthier. That was when I knew I was close to uncovering the truth."

"Even if Reginald and Sir Gerald were involved in an unscrupulous investment scheme," Inspector Finchley said, "Reginald has an alibi. He went home. He can't be the killer."

"Reginald could have taken a taxi," Dirk said. "His home is a five-minute drive from the cricket ground. I don't think he went home to get his heart medication."

"We've checked with his doctor, and he is on medication for a heart condition," Sergeant Matthers said.

"Did you look in his pockets after the murder happened? If his condition is that serious, he should carry his pills at all times," Dirk said.

"We're not in the habit of patting down people for no reason," Inspector Finchley replied.

DEATH AT THE JOLLY CRICKETER 185

I held back a sharp retort. That had nothing to do with it. Inspector Finchley had been afraid to tackle the upper class and ask awkward questions for fear of a backlash.

Dirk shrugged. "Reginald had enough time to get home and return to the cricket ground and kill Sir Gerald. He gave himself an alibi by making a show of being at home, so his maid would see him. But I have another theory about why he left the event."

"What's that?" I asked.

"Reginald and Sir Gerald were neighbours. I think Reginald did go home—"

"We know that!" Inspector Finchley said with utter contempt in his voice. "This is a waste of time."

"Let him speak," I snapped.

Dirk continued, "While Reginald was home, he could easily have snuck into Sir Gerald's house."

"Why on earth would he do that?" Inspector Finchley asked.

"To look for the money," I said. "Reginald knew there was no risk of Sir Gerald catching him because he was at the Jolly Cricketer."

Dirk nodded. "Since Sir Gerald wouldn't return his investment, Reginald decided to take it."

"What nonsense," Inspector Finchley said. "Reginald wouldn't break into another fellow's house."

"He was worried he was about to lose a lot of money," Dirk said. "Fear makes people do unnatural things."

"We must question Reginald again," I said. "As soon as possible. I know you plan to charge Dirk, but it will never stand up in court. Not with such an obvious suspect on the loose."

"I promise you, I didn't do this," Dirk said. "The public would lap up a financial scandal about Sir Gerald's fall from grace. They can't do that now he's dead. Publishing a story about a dead man's financial sneakiness isn't exciting."

"Give me a moment." Inspector Finchley gestured for Sergeant Matthers to follow him out of the room.

I attempted to join them, but Inspector Finchley shook his head, so I remained in my seat.

Dirk turned to me the second the door closed. "I can't thank you enough for supporting me. Inspector Finchley wants me for this crime."

"Inspector Finchley isn't thinking logically," I said. "He's being pressured to close this case. And, of course, his detective chief inspector most likely knows Sir Gerald, Reginald, and most of the chaps who played cricket that day. He wants to protect them."

"He shouldn't be in the job if he's not prepared to bring the law down on anyone who deserves it," Dirk said.

"I know Detective Chief Inspector Taylor," I replied. "He's not pleasant and cares more for the privilege and perks his rank provides than ensuring justice is done."

The door opened, and Inspector Finchley stepped in. "Sergeant Matthers will take you back to your cell."

Dirk gave Benji a final pat and nodded at me as he left the room.

"What shall we do now?" I asked.

"I'd suggest you go about your business," Inspector Finchley replied, "but you'll threaten me with Lady M if I do. So, we're going to Reginald's house."

"You're taking me with you?"

"Better that than you heading off on your own and causing chaos. We're leaving now. I won't wait for you. And you're not bringing the dog."

I dashed after Inspector Finchley, with Benji trotting beside me. "I'm glad you've seen sense."

"I always see sense." He kept his gaze fixed ahead as he walked briskly, most likely hoping I wouldn't keep up. However, he didn't know I could walk for hours with Benji at a faster pace than this.

"What will you say to Reginald when you question him?" I asked.

"We're not speaking to the gentleman." He slid me a glare from the corner of his eye. "I want to see how easy it is to access Sir Gerald's house from Reginald's garden."

"That makes sense. And Reginald is in excellent physical health. He could easily scale fences and walls. Maybe even shimmy up a drainpipe."

"He has a heart condition! That's not a fabrication."

"Yet he regularly plays cricket. I'm sure he could leap about if required to get what he needed. Especially if there was a large sum of money he was worried about losing."

"Let's gather the evidence before we make unfounded assumptions."

I was excited about the prospect of being officially involved in this case. At last, Inspector Finchley saw me as an asset rather than a nuisance.

We hurried outside, Sergeant Matthers joining us after ensuring Dirk was safely back in his cell.

"That thing is not getting in my car." Inspector Finchley pointed at Benji.

"He won't make a peep," I said. "Benji is well-trained. He knows not to distract the driver."

"Absolutely not! My allergies. Of course, if you don't want to come with us…" Inspector Finchley strode to the vehicle's passenger side.

"There's a taxi rank round the corner," Sergeant Matthers said. "Follow us."

I thanked him and dashed off. It felt like I was in a spy novel as I told the cabbie to follow the police car.

We arrived at Reginald's home in Ealing together and parked a short distance from an Edwardian house, with red brick and white stone. Ornate wooden trim details showcased large bay windows, and there was a solid oak door with stained glass inserts.

Sergeant Matthers whistled as we stood looking at the building. "You'd need to spend more than a few pounds to get your hands on a place like this."

"Let's see if there's an easy way to get from one house to the next," I said.

Inspector Finchley pretended he hadn't heard me. "Sergeant, you take the left passage beside the house, and I'll go down the right."

I opted to go with Sergeant Matthers and trailed close behind him with Benji. The passageway was wide, separating the house from its neighbours. At the end of the passage, it opened onto a vast expanse of neatly tended lawn and manicured bushes.

"It must take forever to keep this looking pristine," Sergeant Matthers said. "All I've got is a tiny patch of concrete. Still, I can't complain. It's nice to sit in the sun and have forty winks."

"It sounds perfect. And I agree. What a waste of space. They could build another house on this greenery." I inspected the wall separating the two gardens. It was low enough to hop over, which I demonstrated to Sergeant Matthers. Benji followed, repeating the action several times, thinking it was a game.

"This gate is also unlocked," Sergeant Matthers said. "That's another option to gain access to next door."

"Stop doing that!" Inspector Finchley was looking at me as he marched over. "Someone will see you."

"We were testing how easy it was for Reginald to access Sir Gerald's house," I said.

"Access to the garden, perhaps," Inspector Finchley replied. "But not to the house."

"Let's see how far he took it," I said. "Perhaps Sir Gerald wasn't particular about security."

Inspector Finchley hissed at me to stop, but I hurried towards Sir Gerald's house with Benji at my side. I tried several windows, and they slid up with ease. There was even a back door unlocked. I peered inside. The place felt empty, though there'd be at least a housekeeper in residence.

Male voices reached me, and I tensed. They weren't coming from the house but from the other side of the low wall. I hurried back and found Reginald in his garden. He looked furious to find us poking about.

"I won't stand for this!" he said to Inspector Finchley. "You've had all the information from me. And you've caught the killer!"

"I'm ever so sorry, sir." Inspector Finchley visibly cringed. "I assure you we mean no harm."

"You're breaking your own laws, man!" Reginald snapped. "And what's she doing in Gerald's garden?"

I leapt over the wall with Benji in a show of effortless grace, although I caught my toe and Sergeant Matthers had to stop me from falling. "I was attempting to see how easy it was to access Sir Gerald's house. Something we suspect you did when you returned here on the day of the murder to retrieve your pills."

"Whatever are you talking about?"

"You invested money in one of Sir Gerald's schemes," I said. "Did he panic you? Were you worried you'd lose that money? I imagine, when he didn't return it, you took matters into your own hands."

"Veronica, that's enough," Inspector Finchley said. "Reginald is a respected member of the business community."

"Respected or not, he could easily have broken the law," I said. "And if you entered Sir Gerald's house without his permission, we'll find your fingerprints. Perhaps Sergeant Matthers should dust the door. We could have the wrong man for this murder."

Reginald's face paled, and he shot a furtive glance towards Sir Gerald's house. "How much do you know?"

"Everything," I said before Inspector Finchley made a fudge of things and we lost this opportunity.

Reginald huffed out a breath through flared nostrils. "Damn it to hell! The man owed me a small fortune. I wouldn't have given him a penny if I knew his plans!"

Inspector Finchley looked startled at the sudden revelation. "You're admitting to stealing from Sir Gerald?"

"No! Well…" Reginald hesitated then said with defiance, "I took what I could. And I had every right to take it back. It was my money!"

"You weren't able to get all the money?" I asked.

"I invested a substantial sum. There's a safe, but I couldn't gain access."

"So, when you didn't get it all, you returned to the Jolly Cricketer and attacked Sir Gerald," I said.

"Of course not!"

I sucked in a sharp breath. I didn't believe Reginald. We'd finally found the actual killer.

Chapter 18

I checked to see if my desk telephone worked for what felt like the umpteenth time. I was attempting to focus on the obituaries, but I'd expected to hear from the police by now.

Reginald must be guilty of murdering Sir Gerald. He was up to his neck in the financial scam. Reginald was a rotter and had lied to everybody to conceal his true intent, and he'd been prepared to let an innocent man go down for his crime.

"I see you're not doing your job as usual." Bob sauntered over with a pile of newspapers in his arms.

"What tosh!" I said.

He grunted. "I've barely seen you this week. Anyone would think you run the place, given the amount of time you take off whenever it suits your fancy."

I speared him with a withering look. "I'll admit, I have needed flexible working time, but it was all cleared."

"It always is when your uncle is the boss," Bob said.

"If you don't like the situation, there are plenty of factories that would employ a capable chap such as yourself. I heard the fish processing warehouse is looking for night staff."

"Factory work! I'm qualified, and I have the training. I deserve to be here. Unlike some people."

"Did you miss the module about manners and diplomacy when learning to become a journalist?"

"I only forget that training when I'm around you." He dumped the newspapers on my desk.

"If you expect me to file those, you'll be sorely disappointed," I said.

"We need some dull bits about happy couples. The readers lap up stories about golden wedding anniversaries and love's young dream."

"Why can't you do it?"

"I'm leading on the Jolly Cricketer article. The piece should be written by now, but no thanks to you, we don't have all the information," Bob said. "You're hiding things from me."

"I've disclosed everything I know," I said.

"I don't believe you," Bob said.

"Try harder. Or will that make your brain hurt?"

"I'll use my police contacts if I have to. And if I find out you've been sneakily withholding information, hoping to get a joint byline, there'll be trouble."

"I shall look forward to your trouble," I said.

"And I shall look forward to you staying late to sort through that lot. It'll make up for all the time you've taken off."

Benji emerged from underneath my desk, growling at Bob until he scampered away.

"Good boy. He's such an irritating man," I muttered to Benji. "Uncle Harry gave him this wedding job, but he's foisted it on me because he thinks it's beneath him."

Benji rested a paw on my knee and gently whined.

"Don't worry. We'll treat ourselves to a fish and chip supper once we're finished."

I spent ten minutes flicking through the newspaper articles. Some were decades old. They must have been pulled from the archive. The brides and grooms were so young, many marrying before they turned twenty. I couldn't imagine such a thing. I'd changed so much since my youth.

I paused at a photograph, surprised to recognise several faces among the wedding party.

"Veronica, have you got a moment?" Uncle Harry called out.

I set down the newspapers and headed into his office.

"Bob has just telephoned me from his desk," Uncle Harry said with a sigh. "He accused you of being stubborn and hiding information so he wouldn't make his deadline for the Jolly Cricketer scoop."

"Bob is a well-known nincompoop and a coward since he didn't want to walk past my desk to reach you," I said. "This newspaper gains nothing from me hiding information."

"Go easy on him. I know he can rankle, but he means well."

"Not when it concerns me," I said. "And you know my character. I wouldn't hide information out of spite."

"Exactly! We'll have a front-page exclusive about the deranged slayer in time for printing."

"Deranged slayer sounds so scandalous," I said.

"Unfortunately, we need to bend towards the scandal now and again," Uncle Harry said. "We must sell more newspapers since we're expanding."

"I suppose so," I said. "How's it all going? The expansion plans. Making progress?"

"It's going splendidly. Which is why I want to talk to you," Uncle Harry said. "How do you feel about a move?"

"To a different section of the newspaper? I rather enjoy the obituaries. Please don't say I'm to cover weddings, too?"

"I was speaking more literally. A move to Kent." Uncle Harry paused, taking in my reaction. "It would give you more time with Jacob. I know you've got your office down there, and you're working on the project with your dogs' charity. It would make life easier."

"Oh! I don't know about that." I sank into the chair opposite Uncle Harry. "My home is London. Mother and Matthew are here. They can't do without me."

"I don't like to think of you going back and forth on the train. The effort of managing everything will tear you apart."

"I've thought it out," I said. "I'm working with the dogs' home to find a suitable location in Kent, but I won't volunteer there. Of course, I'd do my bit to promote it, but my loyalty is with the Battersea home. And as for Jacob and the private investigation work, he's in charge."

"You don't mind that?"

I leaned forward. "I'll let you in on a little secret. I never intended to open a business, but when Jacob was injured and the police let him go in such a shocking fashion, I needed to give him a purpose."

"You opened a business to give him something to do?"

"And to make him happy. Jacob means a lot to me."

"You'll barely see each other if he's in Kent and you're in London," Uncle Harry said.

"As I was saying recently about my parents' marriage, a healthy amount of time apart did them the world of good."

Uncle Harry looked bemused. "Why do you say that?"

"They were always glad to see each other," I said. "Father would head off to explore a new pub, and Mother would occupy herself with her children, her hobbies, and her friends. That way, they always had plenty to discuss when they reunited."

Uncle Harry didn't seem convinced. "I doubt that arrangement would have saved my marriage."

"Perhaps not." I worried about Uncle Harry being on his own. He was work-obsessed like me, but what would happen when he retired? "Thank you for the offer, but now is the wrong time to make a big move. Life already feels ... unsettled."

"There's no trouble between you and Jacob, is there?"

"No! We're getting along wonderfully," I said. "But I am missing Ruby."

"She's still not shown her face?"

"There's been no word from her," I said. "And if I moved to a different part of the country, she'd be heartbroken. She said once she wouldn't mind me being in Kent, but it wouldn't be the same."

"You can't always do things to please other people," Uncle Harry said. "You need to make yourself happy, too."

"I genuinely am. Yes, life is stressful, but I'm handling things," I said. "Perhaps you could make the offer to Bob. A change of scene could be the making of him."

"Bob will never leave this office. He'll be carried out of here with his toes up," Uncle Harry said.

"Staying here is the right thing for me. Although things could be changing at home, so I might not be needed."

"What's going on?" Uncle Harry asked.

"Has my mother not told you about her gentleman caller?"

His eyebrows shot up. "Not a word."

"I'm certain I mentioned him. We met Colonel Basil when on holiday in Margate. He's been eager to continue the acquaintance. He's visiting soon."

"This man is sweet on Edith?"

"Yes! I'm as surprised as you," I said. "But they like each other."

Uncle Harry stood from his seat. "I don't agree with that."

I looked up at him in surprise. "Why ever not? Mother gets lonely. She has Matthew for company during the day, but it's not the same as having a husband."

Uncle Harry choked on the coffee he'd sipped on. "There's talk of marriage?"

"Heavens, no! But I see no problem with her having a male companion."

"Your mother's health is fragile." Uncle Harry thumped down his coffee cup. "Won't this be too stressful for her?"

"She is fretful about the situation, and I think she feels guilty about betraying Father's memory, but Colonel Basil is kind and thoughtful. It's just what she needs. And Matthew is keeping a sharp eye on the situation to ensure everything is acceptable."

Uncle Harry shook his head. "It seems wrong."

"Don't you want her to be happy?"

He sighed and pressed his lips together. "It's not that. I'll always think of Edith as Davey's wife. My sister-in-law. The thought of someone else filling Davey's shoes feels ... odd."

"It's a friendship," I said. "Nothing more. Perhaps you should meet Colonel Basil to remove any concerns."

"Yes, I suppose I should. But that's a business for another time." Uncle Harry gestured for me to leave the office, looking more stressed than when I entered. "Get me something on those marriage stories by the end of tomorrow."

This time, it was my turn to sigh. "I suppose it makes a change from death."

"I can always rely on you to come through."

I left his office, puzzled by Uncle Harry's reluctance that my mother had a new gentleman caller. After all, she'd been a widow for some time. A few decades ago, people would have frowned upon her having another companion, but times changed, and I was glad of it.

I settled at my desk again and looked through the wedding photographs once more. I stopped at a group wedding photograph and scanned the names. Aha! I knew I recognised those faces.

There were notable figures from society, including a much younger Lady M, her friend Lady Valentine, and several esteemed earls and countesses. The text also mentioned the Harcourt and Langton families.

It was a wedding uniting the Weaver and Smithson families. Juliet Smithson was marrying Clement Weaver.

That could be Finella and Eleanor's father. Finella had the surname Weaver, and I recalled Lady M and Lady

Valentine discussing the wedding during the cricket event.

It could be an interesting story. I'd make an appointment with Eleanor and Finella to see how the marriage fared and if they had interesting stories to share about their parents. While I was there, I'd see if I could find more nails to hammer into Reginald's coffin to ensure he went down for Sir Gerald's murder.

After making a telephone call to arrange a meeting with Eleanor and Finella the next day, I identified several more families to speak to about their marriages.

I rounded off my afternoon writing a fascinating obituary about a man who met his end by eating wild mushrooms that caused him to hallucinate. He walked in front of a London bus without a stitch of clothing on.

All in all, it had been a jolly good day.

Chapter 19

I dashed out of the house swiftly the next morning. My mother was in a flap because Colonel Basil was due later that day. She was yelling that the house was a mess and needed to be cleaned from top to toe before he could be allowed in, and a puppy had left something unmentionable in a slipper.

Matthew gestured for me to escape while I could, and for that, I was grateful. Perhaps Uncle Harry was right, and Colonel Basil's attentions would be too stressful for my mother to cope with.

My car had been returned the previous evening, so I grabbed Benji, and we drove half an hour to the fashionable quarter of Chelsea to meet Eleanor and Finella.

Due to the surprisingly light traffic, I was fifteen minutes early for my appointment, and despite ringing the front doorbell, no one answered.

I considered walking down the street but decided instead to head along the passageway to the back of the house. Perhaps Eleanor was in the garden, given the unseasonally pleasant weather.

I didn't go far before I heard female voices.

"But I feel terrible!"

"You shouldn't. This will blow over soon, and things will return to normal. Stop flapping about and turning everything into a drama."

I cocked my head. It sounded like Eleanor and Finella. And from Finella's sharp tone, she was irritated with her sister.

"I don't flap! That's unfair," Eleanor said.

"We just need to wait things out, and then we'll go to France," Finella snapped. "The dust will settle, and everyone will forget this nasty business."

"France! Charles would never allow that."

"He'll have no choice, or I'll deal with him," Finella replied.

"Don't you dare! I'm in enough trouble already."

"Trouble of your own making. You only have yourself to blame for not being content with your lot. It'll do you good to keep out of the public eye. Learn to like the quiet life."

"I'll be bored," Eleanor whined.

"Better bored than painted as a scarlet lady and bring even more shame to this family."

Benji lurched forward as a glorious male peacock came into view. The peacock screeched when he spotted Benji and flapped away on his ineffective wings.

"Whatever's going on out here?" Finella's voice sounded dangerously close, so I turned and dashed back to the front of the house, where I rang the bell again and took a few deep breaths to calm myself.

What shame were they talking about? Why did Finella think they should leave the country? What dust needed to settle? Was it because Eleanor's affair with Sir Gerald had been discovered and there was fear of family ruin?

We lived in modern times. People never approved of an affair, but most couples struggled through it without complete ruination.

The front door opened, and a smartly presented butler led me into a back parlour with high ceilings adorned with intricate plasterwork and a crystal chandelier. Plush, velvet draperies in a deep burgundy framed tall, arched windows, and a grand piano sat in one corner.

While I waited for Eleanor and Finella, I inspected the vast collection of books. She had everything from the Brontës to Nietzsche.

"They're for show," Eleanor said as she appeared in the doorway, Finella behind her.

"You have a glorious collection of books," I said.

"Our father was the collector." Eleanor gestured for me to sit at a smartly appointed table by the window with a pleasant view. "I barely have time for reading. Finella reads, though."

Finella settled herself on a nearby sofa and picked up some embroidery. She nodded when her name was mentioned.

"Thank you for seeing me at such short notice," I said. "This assignment was last minute, so I hope I'm not imposing."

"I told you as much as I can recall about our parents' wedding, but second-hand memories are never accurate," Eleanor replied. "Finella has paperwork you might be interested in."

Finella went to a desk, pulled open a drawer, and extracted photographs and documents.

I nodded my thanks as she passed them to me before returning to her embroidery.

"They were married for over thirty years," Finella said.

"They looked blissfully happy on their wedding day," I said.

"It was a marriage of arrangement rather than love," Eleanor said. "At least to begin with, but they became friendly. Considering the two of us are here, they must have been a particular type of friendly. And Finella arrived exactly nine months after the wedding!"

"You shouldn't say such things," Finella muttered.

"I noticed several influential families attended the wedding," I said.

"Our mother's ancestors made their money in textiles, but our father's bloodline can be traced to royalty. Although he worked in finance. Old money has power, even when it's fading," Eleanor said. "I pay little attention to any of it."

Finella grunted her disapproval at the conversation topic.

"Sir Gerald was in finance, wasn't he?" I asked.

"He was. It was such terribly dull dealings. I'd lose interest when he spoke about his business affairs," Eleanor said.

"Is that how he became acquainted with Reginald Harcourt?"

"How is that relevant to your wedding article?" Finella asked.

"It's not. But I thought you'd both be interested to know Reginald is now the prime suspect in Sir Gerald's murder. The police discovered they were involved in a financial scandal."

"We don't need to know about that," Finella said sharply. "That's none of our concern. You're here to ask about our parents' marriage, so let's focus on wedded bliss, shall we?"

"Not that you'd know anything about that." Eleanor's tone turned cutting. "My poor dear sister was jilted at the altar, not once, but twice. Such a shame."

"Don't talk about my personal business!" Finella's cheeks flamed as she stabbed at her embroidery with a tiny silver needle.

"I'm sorry to hear that." I flinched at the anger radiating from Finella as she glared at Eleanor. "Men can be fickle creatures."

"They were only ever in it for the money," Eleanor confided, ignoring Finella's glare. "But no matter the size of the dowry, my sister's hand wasn't suitable."

"Miss Vale has heard enough!" Finella tossed aside her embroidery and stood abruptly. "Let me show you out."

"Oh! Very well. May I keep the photographs and clippings?"

"You may. But be sure to return them."

"We haven't had tea." Eleanor's eyes glinted with mischief. "And I have so much to share with Miss Vale."

"There's no time for tea. We have things to do." Finella ushered me out of the parlour.

I murmured thanks as Finella swiftly showed me out, Benji trotting beside me. She shut the door before I could issue a goodbye.

"Well, I never." I looked back at the house as I reached my car.

It would appear that every family had secrets it didn't want to share, no matter how wealthy they were.

Chapter 20

Following my visit to Eleanor and Finella, I'd been unable to settle, so I diverted to one of my favourite places: the central archive. It was an enormous repository, containing copies of nearly every newspaper, journal, and periodical published. One could happily lose oneself for days in such a place. It was a shame they didn't provide sandwiches and tea, or I'd happily do so.

And with a little gentle bribing involving a tin of shortbread, I could bring Benji in with me.

He was curled in his favourite spot, close to the warm air heater, while I sat hunched over a pile of newspapers. It had taken me time, as I didn't know the exact dates of the weddings, but I'd discovered Finella had indeed been jilted twice. Several notable newspapers printed the details.

The planned weddings had only been a year apart, so Finella or, more likely, her parents had been determined to get her married. Being the eldest sister, they'd have wanted her married before Eleanor. It was an outdated belief, and one I was glad was fading into obscurity, but traditional families clung to the old ways.

The articles didn't detail why the marriages hadn't gone ahead, but I intended to find out. Finella had been a different creature in her own home. And the way she'd spoken to Eleanor when she thought no one could overhear led me to believe there was more to her buttoned-up demeanour than she let on.

After speaking to the clerk and returning the newspapers, I headed to the relevant council office to check the electoral register for contact information. I'd only been able to find details about one of the men Finella had been engaged to. Percival Parker, a local solicitor.

That was a start. He would know about the other man Finella planned to marry, or perhaps I could get all the information I needed from Percival.

Mr Parker lived in an affluent London suburb, along a tree-lined street, although at this time of year, the trees stretched their spindly brown fingers over the pavements, deep in hibernation as they awaited spring.

It wasn't polite to call on a stranger without an invitation, but I would have to sidestep decorum because of my desire to move with haste.

I strode with purposeful intent to his front door and knocked. A handsome, harried-looking chap in his late thirties opened it.

His expression grew puzzled after he took a second to examine me. "Am I expecting you?"

"No, but I'm hoping I have the right house. Are you Percival Parker?" I asked.

"I am. If you run the local Women's Institute and are seeking a donation, you've come to the wrong place."

"Sir! I'm hardly old enough to be part of the Women's Institute!"

He squinted at me. "My apologies. I'm not wearing my spectacles. You're here because…"

I made the introductions, being sure to include Benji. "I'd like to talk to you about your former fiancée, Finella."

He visibly paled and shook his head. "I'm dreadfully busy. And I haven't spoken to Finella in some time."

"It'll only take a few minutes," I said. "Finella has found herself in an unfortunate situation, and I'm seeking clarity to see if I can clear things up."

"Clarity about what?"

I pointedly looked past his shoulder. I didn't want to have this conversation on his doorstep.

Percival sighed. "Come in. But I really am in a hurry. I'm preparing for a case. This is the only place that allows me some peace to put together my final thoughts."

"I understand you're in the legal profession." I followed him along a neat hallway and into the back parlour, which was competently decorated in dark colours and vintage accessories.

"Did Finella tell you that?" Percival asked.

"No, but you're a notable figure in this community." Perhaps flattery would get him to drop his guard. I wasn't adept at it, but with Ruby still absent, I'd give it a whirl.

"If you say so." He offered me a seat and settled opposite me on a plaid sofa.

"I'll be brief," I said as I settled Benji on the floor. "Finella and her sister, Eleanor, recently attended a charity cricket match at a pub I own. The Jolly Cricketer."

His eyebrows flicked up, and he nodded for me to continue.

"Unfortunately, a man was murdered at the event. You may have read about it in the newspaper. Sir Gerald Langton."

"Gosh! Murder? I can't say I know the fellow or read the article. What a terrible business. And I know of the Jolly Cricketer. It's in a respectable part of town. You can't imagine something like that happening in such a solid neighbourhood."

"Indeed. It was a shock for all of us," I said.

Percival tilted his head. "What does this have to do with me?"

"It's a delicate matter," I said.

He scrubbed his forehead with his fingers. "Good grief! Are you suggesting Finella and Sir Gerald were together when he died?"

"No! But it involves an affair of the heart, of sorts," I said. "I wanted to ask why your relationship with Finella didn't result in marriage."

"Ah. That's a personal question." Percival's tone remained cautious. "And it's also none of your business."

"I apologise for the intrusive nature of my words, but Lady M has engaged me to look into this matter."

"Lady M! Do you mean Lady Marie Antoinette Montague-Fortense-Denburgh?"

"The very same."

"You move in interesting circles. My, my. Did you say your surname is Vale?"

I nodded.

"I don't know your family. Pubs, you say?"

"That's correct. Lady M attended the charity event," I said. "It's only natural she wants to know what happened."

Percival sat silently for several seconds, his gaze fixed on the window. "Do you think Finella was involved in what happened to Sir Gerald?"

I hesitated. "Someone struck him down with considerable violence. The police are certain a man did it, and so was I. Until recently."

"What changed your mind?" Percival's sharp gaze settled on me.

"I got to know Finella's character, and it set me to wondering," I said. "When you were together, were you ever concerned about your safety?"

Percival's cheeks flushed. "I can look after myself in any situation. I boxed at Oxford."

I remained silent.

He sighed. "I didn't propose to Finella because I loved her, but I'm assuming you know that. When I was younger, I had an ambitious career plan. Unfortunately, my family fell on hard times, and they couldn't support me at a crucial juncture."

"And Finella has her own fortune," I said.

"It was why I made her acquaintance," Percival admitted. "It wasn't my proudest moment, but I was desperate. My father died and left us in a dreadful mess. He made unwise investments, which we realised too late. My mother was racked with grief and barely able to function. I needed to save the family home and ensure my mother and four sisters weren't put out on the street."

"You proposed to Finella, and she accepted," I said. "What made you change your mind?"

"I thought I'd be able to manage Finella," he said. "When we met, she was subdued. She barely said a word or glanced at me. I was a young man full of arrogance. I decided I'd marry this quiet creature, set her up in a smart London home, and leave her to potter around. I'd be busy making a name for myself. And…"

I pursed my lips. "You'd find a woman with more fire. And thanks to Finella's money, you'd have enough to set them both up."

"As I mentioned, I was a young man with too much ego. But … then something happened. Well, more than one thing."

"It must have been significant to make you call off the wedding and lose access to Finella's fortune."

"Yes, it was rather." Percival looked at the floor. "My family had a spot of good news. Not all of my father's investments failed. One came good. It provided us with enough money to secure the house and a few years of income. It also brought me time to complete my training and set up in business."

"You no longer needed Finella's money, so you broke off the engagement," I said.

"No! That wasn't the reason. We would have got by, but the existence would have been frugal," Percival said. "I still planned on marrying the girl."

My eyes widened a fraction. "What happened?"

"Finella changed. I caught a glimpse or two of a different character when she didn't think anyone was watching. I thought she was seeing what boundaries she'd be living in. It was more than that. Finella was playing a part. And I discovered that to my cost."

"She was unkind to you?" I asked.

"More than unkind. I can't believe I'm telling you this, but ... she attacked me!"

"She struck you?"

His cheeks flushed red. "We were discussing living arrangements. I suggested she might like a home of her own, where I wouldn't be in the way. She grew furious and said she'd be a laughingstock if her husband didn't live with her."

"You can understand any woman being unhappy about that situation," I said. "Finella may have cared deeply for you."

"She didn't. She was sweet enough when we were in company, but the second we were alone, she ignored me. She was curt. Sometimes unpleasant. Finella behaved as if she wanted nothing to do with me."

"Which suited you," I said. "You were marrying her for her money, not her affection."

"Yes! And perhaps we could have rubbed along as friends, but she wasn't interested. She said she knew what my game was and wouldn't stand for it. She laid out her own rules about my expected behaviour and made it clear there'd be no opportunity for a mistress. It was all very shocking."

"Some may consider taking a mistress shocking."

"Finella understood it was a marriage of convenience. For both of us. Her parents wanted her gone. I wanted the money. It could have worked." Percival's voice lowered. "I set down my own rules. That was when she grabbed a poker by the fireplace and whacked me with it. Repeatedly! She seemed intent on doing me in."

My unsettled feelings about Finella intensified. If she hid a violent streak, it could have resurfaced at the Jolly

Cricketer. If she'd learned about Eleanor's affair with Sir Gerald, she could have confronted him, demanding he cut off the relationship. They ended up in the cellar, and she struck him. Perhaps she hadn't intended to kill him, but that was the outcome.

"I'm only telling you this because of the other poor fellow," Percival said.

"To whom are you referring? Sir Gerald?"

"No. The other man Finella intended to marry."

"I couldn't find out much about him."

"You wouldn't. He's been dead for five years!"

"From natural causes?"

"No. Someone shot him!"

I drew in a sharp breath. "Did the police find out who did it?"

"Not as far as I know," Percival said. "Of course, they spoke to me since I'd been engaged to Finella, and they thought I might harbour feelings for her and want the other chap out of the way, but I couldn't tell them anything. I'd called off the engagement after Finella attacked me. I'd rather my family live frugally than deal with that! And I was glad I did. I had chills for days when I learned the other chap she almost walked down the aisle with was murdered."

My mind whirled with this information. I had to know Finella's exact movements during the charity lunch. She'd admitted she left to get air, but what if she'd gone outside to put to work her plot to get rid of Sir Gerald?

"I'm sorry if I've unsettled you, but since you were questioning Finella's character, I thought it would be helpful," Percival said. "Would you like a brandy to settle the nerves?"

"No, thank you. May I use your telephone? I need to contact the police."

"You really are involved in this puzzle!" Percival showed me to the telephone in the hallway and left me alone as I quickly telephoned Sergeant Matthers.

"There's no news," he said after I'd asked about Reginald. "He isn't confessing to the murder. But he has confessed to fraud, so we've got him on that."

"And the killer?" I asked. "Who is Inspector Finchley focused on?"

"He's still looking at Dirk. But there's a problem. We've had the results back on the false leg. There's no damage or any traces of blood on it."

"I knew it wasn't Dirk," I said. "But I've learned something worrying about Finella. Did you know she had two failed engagements?"

There was a shuffling sound as Sergeant Matthers must have been flipping through his notes. "I have no record of that. I don't think we asked about her relationships, only her current situation."

"A man she was engaged to was shot dead, and she attacked the other chap with a fire poker. He was so scared of her, he called off their engagement."

"Well, I never!" Sergeant Matthers said. "To be honest, we didn't look closely at Finella. Her sister was her alibi, and we could find no connection between Sir Gerald and Finella."

"She had an opportunity."

"But no motive," Sergeant Matthers said. "Finella told us she didn't know the victim."

"Finella has been lying, and not just to us," I said. "We need to find out exactly what she got up to on the day Sir Gerald was murdered."

Chapter 21

All members of staff who'd served at the Jolly Cricketer during the charity event stood before me. Several looked nervous at meeting their employer's employer, although one or two of the young men appeared bored. Cedric had swiftly assembled them, so I could question the staff about Finella's movements.

"As you all know, there was a recent tragedy during a charity event," I said. "Sadly, the police keep attempting to charge the wrong people with the crime, so I've taken matters into my own hands."

"Are you planning to solve it for them?" one of the young men asked, a cheeky grin on his face.

"You watch your tongue," Cedric said. "It won't be the first time Miss Vale has helped the police. She's smart and has a quick mind."

"Thank you, Cedric. We must ensure justice is done. The way the police are handling things, I fear for the outcome." I studied the group and was happy I now had their full attention. "Information has emerged to suggest a new suspect. But I need your help to get to the truth."

"How can we help?" a waitress asked.

"I'm interested in the movements of a lady at the event," I said. "She attended with Eleanor Pembroke. She's her older sister, Finella."

"I remember Mrs Pembroke," the cheeky young man said. "She's a cracker."

"I remember her sister," Cedric said. "She wasn't friendly. Not one for small talk. She came to the bar several times, complaining service was too slow. We worked as fast as we could, and no one else complained."

"I also met Finella at the bar," I said. "I appreciate everyone thinking carefully about her movements that afternoon. This is crucial."

The group mumbled to each other, no one keen on being the spokesperson.

"Someone needs to speak up," Cedric said. "You've all got eyes. You should pay attention to the guests when you're working."

A plain-faced girl of around eighteen stepped forward. "I saw her leave. More than once. Sometimes, it was for five minutes, and then she'd return to the table."

"Finella would always go outside when she left the table?" I asked.

"I watched her through the window. She went to the shops opposite the pub but didn't go inside. She ducked into the alley. I wondered what she was doing."

"Perhaps she had a fella tucked away back there," a young man quipped. "She kept nipping out to grab a sneaky kiss."

The group laughed.

"Or Finella was waiting for an opportunity," I murmured to myself. "Did anyone else see Finella leave the event?"

There were several nods.

"What about going into the cellar?"

No one admitted to seeing that. Finella must have been sneaky, picking her moment to slip into the cellar. But how had she encouraged Sir Gerald to join her down there?

"Thank you. You've been most helpful," I said. "Keep up the good work."

Cedric dismissed the group and joined me, feeding Benji a biscuit from his apron pocket. "Watch yourself. If this lady harmed Sir Gerald and she thinks you're on to her, she won't think twice about doing the same to you."

"Finella doesn't know I suspect her of murder," I said. "I've informed the police, although Inspector Finchley is still keen on charging somebody else. Since he's paying me no attention, I must act. I refuse to allow an innocent man to be charged with murder."

"I don't like to think of you looking into this alone," Cedric said.

"I have my trusty companion by my side. He always watches out for me." I patted Benji on the head. "How's business?"

"Couldn't be brisker. Everyone wants to talk about what happened. I've even had a few people try to slip me money to take them on a tour of the murder site. Have you ever heard of such a thing?"

"Sadly, I have. Thank you for keeping everything under control."

"Of course. And I owe you a debt."

I arched an eyebrow. "Literally and figuratively."

Cedric blushed. "I'll never forget you let me keep this job. I did you wrong, and most people wouldn't be able to forgive that."

"We're all allowed to make mistakes. It's what we do after the fact that is most important."

"I appreciate that. What do you intend to do now?" Cedric followed us to the main door and opened it.

"Continue gathering evidence until I have enough to convince the police they're holding the wrong person."

We said our goodbyes, and I checked the road was clear of traffic before dashing across it with Benji. I entered the store directly opposite, which was a smartly turned-out tobacconist and sweet shop.

The owner was no help. He couldn't remember seeing Finella enter the shop or go along the alleyway beside it.

"There'd be no reason someone would want to go down there," he said. "You can't get out the other side. It got blocked off a few years back. We use it to store the rubbish until it's collected. Are you sure the lady in question went down there?"

I nodded. "Would you mind if I looked along the alleyway?"

The shop owner looked askance. "It's not tidy. As I said, it's where we store all our rubbish."

"I want to see if there's any reason she went down there."

He still looked doubtful. "So long as you don't mind getting those smart shoes grubby."

I smiled. "I have no qualms about muddy shoes. I'll take a two-penny bag of mint chocolate creams before I go."

With my sweets in hand, I left the shop with Benji, and we walked into the alley. There was a slight smell of dampness and several large bins.

I looked around the bins and walked to the end of the alley. As described, a high brick wall prevented any exit. You couldn't climb over it. I stepped away from the wall, walking backwards slowly, my gaze covering every brick. Benji remained at the end of the alley close to the wall, having discovered a fascinating smell that consumed him.

"What were you doing here, Finella?" I whispered. "Hoping to catch Sir Gerald unawares? Did you think he might leave the event and you could tackle him outside?"

Benji kept sniffing, and I kept looking.

"It didn't work, though, did it?" I continued. "You had to return to the Jolly Cricketer and risk everything to get Sir Gerald into the cellar. How did you do it?"

There was a scuffle behind me. Before I could turn, something hard pressed into the small of my back.

"You're too clever for your own good." It was Finella. "Don't move. I've got nothing left to lose, so I'm not afraid to pull the trigger."

Benji growled and stalked towards us.

"I'll shoot him!" Finella said. "Call your dog off and tell him to keep quiet."

I gulped down my panic and gestured for Benji to sit.

He wasn't happy about the instruction because he could see I was in trouble, but he was an obedient dog.

"How did you know I'd be here?" I asked.

"You needed watching, so that's what I've been doing. You can't expect to come into my home and pull the wool over my eyes," Finella said. "I saw you when you first arrived. Then you disappeared. It was your dog that startled the peacock, wasn't it?"

"Peacock?" Drat. I'd thought we'd been speedy enough not to be spotted.

"He's a useful alarm for when we're in the garden. I knew something had startled him when he kicked up a storm and shot off. It was you. Snooping. You overheard our conversation, didn't you?"

"If you remove the gun from my back, we could have a more civilised conversation," I said.

"That's not happening."

"People will hear if you pull the trigger in such a populated area."

"It's too late for me to care about such a thing," Finella said.

"Because you're guilty of murdering Sir Gerald?"

"Him? Why waste my time on him?"

"There are plenty of reasons," I said. "And I have witnesses who saw you leave your table at the charity cricket event several times."

Finella tutted in my ear. "What did that wet sop of a former fiancé say to you?"

"How did you know I met Percival?"

"Like I said, I've been following you. Did he tell you I'm an awful woman and he couldn't marry me?"

"We had an enlightening conversation," I said. "He admitted you were abusive towards him."

"Abusive? I'm a woman! We're always neglected or poorly treated by men." Her hot breath slid past my cheek. "Did Percival tell you everything? His plans to take a mistress and abandon me in some dull house to act as his unpaid cleaner and nursemaid for the children he'd insist we have?"

"He was forthcoming," I said. "And after hearing you intimidate Eleanor and threaten Charles's life, I knew I was onto something."

"You've got this wrong."

"You didn't leave the cricket match to make arrangements to murder Sir Gerald?"

"I didn't murder him!"

"You despised him because he was having an affair with your sister," I said.

"I didn't approve. Eleanor has an incredible life. Charles gives her everything. But it's never enough. She always demands more. It's only her panic making her act rashly. She thinks once her looks fade, she'll be ignored." Finella grunted. "I know how that feels. I'm the plain one. I'm surprised anyone noticed my movement at the cricket match since I'm the invisible sister."

"I'm sorry people have been unkind to you," I said. "But that's no excuse for murder."

She jabbed the gun into my back, making me wince and Benji growl again.

"Sir Gerald didn't die by my hand," Finella hissed in my ear.

"I suppose you planned on using this gun on him," I said. "But it would have drawn attention if you'd fired inside the pub. You needed him outside but missed your chance to get him."

"A gun is an effective weapon," Finella said. "But I didn't have this gun at the cricket event. I had no reason to have it in my possession."

"Too much of a risk, I suppose," I said. "But a cricket bat. That's a handy weapon. And you're strong."

"As strong as most men," Finella said. "They don't see that as an asset. They think it's unbecoming for a woman to look after herself. Eleanor plays the meek little thing. A damsel in distress. She's not. She's smarter than most men, and she learned ballet from the age of three. She's probably stronger than me."

"You're suggesting Eleanor murdered Sir Gerald?"

"I didn't say that! Stop putting words into my mouth."

"You're each other's alibi. And from this conversation, it's clear neither of you told the truth to the police about your comings and goings at the charity event."

"Sir Gerald was Eleanor's golden goose! She'd never kill him," Finella said. "Leave her out of it."

"I will if you confess," I said.

Finella huffed in my ear. "The police are about to charge somebody, so you'll get no confession from me."

"With the evidence I've gathered, all the other suspects will be let go," I said.

"Not if I claim I saw one of them do it," Finella said. "That would muddy the waters."

"And give you and your sister a chance to escape to France."

Finella sighed. "You heard everything. What a pity. There aren't enough smart women in this world."

"Do you always intimidate your sister?" I asked. "You threaten the people she cares about so she'll obey you?"

"It wasn't a threat! Eleanor is clever, but she refuses to engage her brain," Finella said. "I'm protecting us. We need to get away from the scandal. The gossips will have a field day over the news about her affair. And Charles will divorce her. He won't want to, but he needs to save face. He can't be seen as a cuckolded husband. What will we do then?"

"What about your family's money?"

"Eleanor has spent most of it," Finella said. "I've tucked away a small sum, but it won't be enough for both of us. At least, not the way she wants to live."

"You'll need very little money when serving a sentence," I said.

"Sir Gerald's blood isn't on my hands!"

"We should let the police decide that." I drew in a breath. I did not know how to extract myself from this deadly situation, so I needed to keep Finella talking. "Perhaps he's not the only man you murdered. Percival informed me your other fiancé was shot. By the gun in your hand, perhaps?"

Finella noisily breathed in and out. "My parents insisted I marry. They didn't want me to stay at home. They saw me as a burden. Maybe even an embarrassment."

"They arranged the matches for you?"

"I went along with it. The men were pleasant enough, if dull. But then they let me down. They didn't want me. Only my money. After the second failed attempt, our parents relented and said Eleanor could marry whomever she chose. It was grossly unfair. Eleanor had so much freedom. She'd stay out until all hours, flirting with any man she desired. My parents indulged her. They barely tolerated me."

"It must have been a relief when they died and you were free," I said.

"I thought it would be, but nothing has changed," Finella said. "I'm still the plain spinster, invisible and a burden."

"You funnelled your rage into action. You murdered your former fiancé, didn't you?"

Finella was silent for several heartbeats. "You know the truth now. Others will soon. Eleanor already suspects, but she's kept her silence because she cares for me. It doesn't matter now, so long as I buy myself time."

She removed the gun from my back, allowing me to turn. Finella's gaze was stony as she held the weapon steady.

I refused to allow my panic to take over. It would solve nothing. "What do you plan on doing next?"

"I'm done with living in the shadows. I deserve happiness. But with you in my way, I'll never get it. You're as relentless as I am when you want something."

"You'll never get away with it."

"I will! All I need is extra time and for you to be out of my way for good." Finella sighted the gun on my chest.

Benji leapt just as the gun went off.

Chapter 22

My ears rang from the explosive noise of the weapon firing.

Finella yelped and staggered back as Benji hit her square in the chest. Had the bullet hit Benji? I had no time to consider the grim consequences as I lunged at Finella and tackled her to the ground.

"Lord above! Was that a gun?" Cedric appeared at the entrance to the alleyway.

Finella fired at him, the bullet pinging off the brick close to his head and making him duck.

"Take cover!" I yelled. "And call the police."

I almost lost my grip on Finella's gun hand but dug in my fingernails and reached for the weapon with my free hand. Her grip was iron-tight, but I twisted her arm, forcing it upward so she couldn't shoot anyone. She cried out in pain, her face contorting with rage.

Finella kneed me hard in the stomach, and I gasped, but I refused to let go. The gun wavered between us, too close, too dangerous.

Benji was no longer fighting, and my heart spasmed when I glimpsed him behind Finella. He was down, and there was a smear of red in his fur.

"Let me go!" Finella hissed.

I only tightened my grip, using fear and rage to fuel me. The gun finally clattered free, spinning just out of reach of both of us.

We scrambled for it. My fingers touched the barrel, but Finella yanked me back by the shoulder. I twisted, kicking out, and my boot caught her square in the jaw.

She yelped, clutching her face, and I dove for the gun, snatching it up.

"Stay down!" I shouted, the weapon trembling as I aimed it at her.

Finella sat up slowly, blood trickling from the corner of her mouth. "You won't pull the trigger."

My breath came out in ragged gasps as my gaze flicked from Benji to Finella. "You hurt my dog. He's my closest ally. How dare you!"

She didn't move, her eyes locked on mine. The alley was deathly silent, save for my heart pounding and ringing ears.

We stared at each other, neither daring to blink.

"You're not as like me as I first thought," Finella finally said. "You have too much to lose. That dog. Your friends. Your work. I have nothing. Why not take my revenge on the men who attempted to use me to get what they wanted? That's justice."

"That's not justice. That's spite. You could have stood up to your parents."

"They would have sent me away for speaking my mind. Eleanor is my only friend, even though I vex her." Finella lifted onto one knee. "I could not lose her. I had to accept my lot. You don't know how lucky you are."

"And you don't know how lucky you are that I haven't shot you for hurting Benji." I crouched slowly and checked his breathing. He was still with me.

Finella took a step towards me.

"That's enough! Make another move, and I'll see how rusty my trigger finger is."

Her expression shifted to curious. "You've also killed someone?"

"During the war, I delivered more than the post and cups of tea. I did my bit in every sense of the word."

"I can't believe you've taken another life. Your high and mighty conscience wouldn't allow it." She lunged and slammed into my legs, knocking me down.

Finella grabbed the gun, staggered to her feet, and dashed off. She made it to the end of the alley before stopping. A gasp fell from her lips. She turned and looked back, taking a few steps closer, the gun still in her hand and unhinged hatred burning in her eyes.

I stood frozen, staring at the blood on Benji's fur. He was still alive but panting and clearly in shock. How badly was he injured?

Finella glanced back at her escape route and lowered the gun as hurried footsteps echoed closer. The police were finally here! However, my focus was on making sure Benji survived.

I searched for the bullet wound, being gentle as he whimpered his distress. "I'll save you. No matter what it takes." I wasn't losing Benji.

"My! That all sounds dramatic." Lady M was seated at an ornate desk in one of her many parlours as I updated her on the outcome of the investigation. She was rifling through the drawers, opening and shutting them and sighing.

"Finella is a troubled woman. But everything came right in the end," I said.

Settled beside me on a luxurious sofa, Benji lay snuggled. After my initial shock at discovering him injured, I knew exactly where to get assistance. Lady M had access to the best veterinarians in the country. A telephone call, a private car, and several worrying hours, and he was on the mend.

Fortunately, the bullet only grazed his leg, leaving no serious injuries. After treatment and several days of rest, Benji was enjoying all the attention of being a hero, receiving treats, and basking in the warmth of several woollen blankets gifted by Lady M, along with her own cashmere wrap. He was curled under it, fast asleep.

"There is one sticking point," I said.

Lady M kept rummaging through her desk drawers. "What would that be?"

"Finella refuses to confess to Sir Gerald's murder."

"She killed the other chap, though, didn't she? Her fiancé?"

"Former fiancé," I corrected. "She admitted as much to me, but she keeps insisting she didn't murder Sir Gerald."

"It doesn't matter much either way. The police have her for murder."

"It could be the difference between hanging and a life sentence."

Lady M thumped a drawer shut with a huff.

"Have you lost something?" I asked.

"It would appear so. It's most vexing." She stood and joined me on the sofa, gently stroking Benji's head. "How is he doing?"

"Thoroughly enjoying being spoiled," I said. "I can't thank you enough for your help. Your man in London was excellent. I'll repay every penny."

"You absolutely will not give me anything," Lady M said. "I feel responsible for this. I insisted you get involved in the case."

"You only did that because Inspector Finchley was being such a stubborn-headed ninny," I replied.

"Well, it worked. That foolish fellow was chasing the wrong suspect. It's all thanks to you and the wonderful Benji that the police caught Finella." Lady M lightly patted the back of my hand. "Now, that's enough about you paying me back. I've recently learned a valuable lesson. Never loan friends or family money and expect it to be returned. If you give money, it's a gift, nothing more."

"Does that wisdom pearl relate to what you've been searching for? Loan documentation?"

Lady M leaned back on the sofa, her expression hardening. "I should have been more thorough, but I thought there was nothing to worry about. Lady Valentine is respectable, and we've known each other for more years than I care to admit."

"You lent Lady Valentine money, and she's refusing to return it?"

"She's not only refusing to return it, but she is pretending she never received it. And she's leaving the country!" Lady M said. "She telephoned today to let me know she won't be attending next month's riding event. When I questioned her, she said she had an emergency abroad."

"Why would she forget you've loaned her money?"

"Her memory is as sharp as mine, so I know it is deliberate." Lady M tutted. "It's unbecoming. She must think I won't press on the matter because discussing finances is crass. However, I jotted down what she'd borrowed on a piece of paper, so I know I speak the truth. If only I could find it."

"Perhaps she'll repay you upon her return."

"That's if she returns. She's booked an afternoon passage on a ship that leaves today. And as for the money, my polite requests for its return have been ignored for months. If she leaves these shores for good, I'll never see it again." Lady M huffed out a breath. "I won't miss it. But that is not the point. Friends shouldn't do that to each other."

"How curious. Do you know what the emergency is that's making her leave so swiftly?" I asked.

"Lady Valentine said she had little time to speak and just wanted to let me know out of courtesy. I couldn't get anything else out of her. She's been behaving strangely for several months. Fretting about things."

"Perhaps a problem with her husband," I suggested. "From what Lady Valentine said at the Jolly Cricketer, he's rarely in this country."

"Because she prefers it that way," Lady M said. "Although I've heard a few rumours about him. He's taken a mistress in Spain."

"Maybe he's diverted his funds to support his mistress. Lady Valentine could be feeling the pinch but is too embarrassed to say," I said.

"She may well be," Lady M said. "There has also been a rumour she pawned some jewellery. Can you imagine such a thing? Her family bloodline is as pure and respected as my stallion, Brutus."

"I assumed the Valentine family was eye-wateringly wealthy," I said.

"They used to be. But a few poor deals can topple any empire," Lady M said.

I nodded in agreement and then excused myself to use the toilet.

"Stay out of the Red Room!" Lady M called after me. "I'm having work done in there, so it's unsafe to enter."

I used the bathroom and took a moment to freshen up. What a strange week it had been. Everything was shifting. Mother with her new gentleman friend. Ruby vanishing. Benji injured. Even Lady M was unsettled because of Ruby's absence and Lady Valentine taking her money.

I stopped in the middle of drying my hands on a soft towel. Why hadn't Finella confessed to Sir Gerald's murder? She'd never see freedom again, so she should do the decent thing.

My thoughts flicked to the wedding photographs. Lady Valentine and Lady M were in those photographs. If Lady Valentine moved in the same circles as the Harcourts and the Langtons, was it possible she'd invested in their fraudulent scheme?

And if her husband was no longer financially supporting her because he'd become besotted with an exotic mistress, Lady Valentine could be in financial dire straits. Was that why she'd pawned her jewellery?

I dashed back to the parlour. "Lady M, may I leave Benji with you? He's settled, and I don't want to disturb him."

"He's always welcome. Both of you may stay as long as you like. Although you must stay out of the Red Room. None of your snooping. I know what you are like."

"Thank you," I said. "Do you know which port Lady Valentine will depart from?"

"Southampton. Why ever do you want to know?"

"And what time is she due to depart?"

"The ship sails at six this evening. You're not planning a last-minute flit, too, are you?"

"I'll get back to you on that. I must dash. Thank you again." I kissed the top of Benji's soft head, rushed to my car, and zoomed away.

It all made sense! Finella wasn't confessing to Sir Gerald's murder because she didn't do it.

Chapter 23

I'd made a swift stop before heading to Southampton, telephoning Sergeant Matthers to let him know my concerns.

Naturally, he'd been flabbergasted, but I'd convinced him to meet me in Southampton, along with a contingent from the local police force before Lady Valentine set sail and we never saw her again.

Although I had my car, the train was the faster option. The journey still took over three hours.

Lady M said the ship wouldn't sail until the evening, but it was still a relief to see it docked.

I looked around as I exited the taxi that had brought me to the dock, soon spotting the distinctive black police car used by most forces. I hurried over, and Sergeant Matthers emerged. He introduced me to two of his colleagues from the Hampshire Constabulary.

"Are you sure about this?" Sergeant Matthers asked. "Lady Valentine is an influential sort. If we get this wrong..."

"It all makes sense," I said. "We just need her to come clean."

"I didn't mention this development to Inspector Finchley," Sergeant Matthers said as we hurried to the ship. "Just in case things don't go as planned."

"I'm glad you didn't," I said. "He would never have allowed it."

"He's my superior, so I respect him, but he has his blinders on with the upper classes," Sergeant Matthers said.

"He needs to remove them," I replied. "Did you request a check on Lady Valentine's financial situation?"

"I rushed it through after you telephoned," Sergeant Matthers said. "The bank couldn't give me all the information over the telephone, but they told me there have been problems. The Valentines hold a substantial debt with the bank. One they haven't been making repayments on recently."

"Goodness! Did Lady Valentine bet the entire fortune on Sir Gerald's investment scam?"

"She made several large deposits directly to Sir Gerald," Sergeant Matthers said.

"Lady Valentine must have discovered the fraud. Sir Gerald refused to return the funds, and she grew desperate." I touched Sergeant Matthers's arm. "I know you're in charge but let me speak to Lady Valentine first."

"I hoped you say that. I find myself flustered if a lady of class misbehaves. You can speak plainly to her."

My smile was wry. "I'm known for it."

"I made a telephone call to the transport police who oversee the port," Sergeant Matthers said. "Lady Valentine is being held. They claimed they were doing extra checks on passports. Apparently, she wasn't happy at being delayed."

"I imagine not," I said. "She must be worried the game is up."

We found the relevant room, and a stern-faced policeman who looked a little like the bloodhound currently in the dogs' home led us to where Lady Valentine was being held.

She looked shocked when she saw me. "Miss Vale! Did they haul you in to inspect your passport, too? Are we to be travel companions? It's scandalous. I have never experienced such treatment in my life."

"Perhaps that's because this is the first time you've committed a murder," I said.

Lady Valentine gasped, and the transport policeman looked startled at my bluntness. But we were well past manners and politeness. Benji had been injured in the line of duty while we investigated this case, and that was unforgivable.

"I won't waste anyone's time. You murdered Sir Gerald Langton at the Jolly Cricketer," I said.

"How very dare you!" Lady Valentine said. "I barely knew the man. Why would I kill a stranger?"

"Your connection to the Langton family goes back generations. I discovered a wedding photograph with you in it. You even mentioned you attended the wedding with Lady M. The photograph includes members of the Langton and Harcourt families."

"I have attended dozens of weddings with many influential and well-respected families also receiving an invitation. That means nothing," Lady Valentine said.

"Not on its own," I said. "But I'm curious to know why you must leave the country so quickly."

"It's a personal matter and therefore none of your concern."

"Is it connected to your financial worries?" I pressed.

"Again, absolutely none of your business."

"The police have checked with your bank," I said. "You owe them a significant amount of money, and your accounts are empty. Was that why you pawned your jewellery? You needed to buy a passage out of this country?"

"No funds? Pawning my gems? I have never been so insulted in my life," Lady Valentine said.

"I'm just getting started." The anger and frustration that had built over the past few weeks flooded out. The mystery surrounding my father's death. Ruby's disappearance. Benji's injury. Attempting to balance my professional and private life. It was all too much.

Lady Valentine turned her frosty gaze on Sergeant Matthers. "Where is your superior? I'll have your job for this. And I want Miss Vale arrested."

Sergeant Matthers startled. "On what charge, your ladyship?"

Lady Valentine appeared stunned he was questioning her, rather than snapping to attention and putting me in shackles. "For intruding on my private affairs."

"You have a financial connection to Sir Gerald," I said. "The police know you deposited several large amounts of money directly into his bank account. We're also aware Sir Gerald and Reginald Harcourt, along with most likely several of their friends, devised a scam to take people's money and pretend to invest it into a surefire plan. When it failed, they said there was nothing they could do, and you lost everything."

"I know nothing about that." Lady Valentine glanced around the room. "Someone must have made a mistake transferring the funds. The bank will compensate me for the inconvenience."

"Not if you authorised the transfer," I said. "You must have been furious when you learned your money was lining swindlers' pockets."

Lady Valentine's mouth dropped open. She quickly composed herself and settled her hands into her lap. "Is ... is the money all gone?"

"It's something the police will look into," I said. "Exactly how much did you invest?"

"I'm admitting to nothing," Lady Valentine said.

"You must desperately need financial help," I said. "The accounts are empty. Your husband has a new mistress to finance, and you're pawning your jewels. You're at the end of your tether."

"I have resources. Admittedly, some aren't liquid, so it'll take time to release the funds. Besides, it is cheaper to live abroad."

"You weren't planning on coming back, were you?" I asked. "If you could get to Spain, you'd be out of reach. Provided you never came back to this country, the police couldn't charge you with Sir Gerald's murder."

"No one will charge me with murder because I am innocent," Lady Valentine said.

"Where is your walking cane?" I asked. "The one with the elaborate silver top. I admired it at the charity cricket event."

"I don't always need a cane to walk. Sometimes, my arthritis plays up."

"You don't have the cane with you, because you used it to kill Sir Gerald," I said. "You confronted him at the Jolly Cricketer and demanded your money back. When he refused, you lost control of your temper. You struck him. Perhaps the first blow wasn't enough to kill him, but it confused him enough that you got him into the cellar, where you finished the job."

Lady Valentine looked away. A lengthy silence stretched out.

"These modern times were supposed to bring change," she said. "Positive change for all. During the war, I saw that remarkable change. It was freeing. Not being shackled to a man and relying on him. The world may have been at war, but I was happy. I had a purpose. I could do what I desired."

"And then the war ended, and your husband wanted things to return to the old ways?" I asked.

"I had to find a way out," Lady Valentine said. "But I needed money to do so. My husband controlled our finances. It made me sick. He controlled my money, and I had no say in how he spent it. However, I had an understanding with the bank manager. We agreed to divert funds discreetly. Those funds would grow as Sir Gerald promised, and I would have enough money to leave and live the life I wanted."

"But Sir Gerald deceived you," I said.

Lady Valentine cast a world-weary look at me. "I was desperate to escape."

"And when you tried to rectify the error, Sir Gerald wouldn't listen?"

"He laughed at me!" she exclaimed. "He said I knew the risks, and it was my fault. He dared to call me a foolish woman who had no mind for handling complicated finances."

"That was when you hit him?"

"I was swinging my walking cane at his head before I knew what I was doing. I didn't mean to kill him. But once I'd injured him, I had to make sure he couldn't talk, or my secret would be revealed."

"How did you bundle Sir Gerald down the cellar steps and wallop him?" Sergeant Matthers asked. "Even an injured chap will put up a fight."

"I'm surprisingly strong for a mature woman," Lady Valentine said. "I've ridden horses all my life. I still do. Besides, he was gravely wounded, so he hardly fought back."

"What did you do with your cane?" Sergeant Matthers sounded hushed with shock.

"I hid it," Lady Valentine said.

"We already have enough evidence to charge you," I said. "Show willingness to cooperate, and the judge will appreciate it."

"I know every judge in London," Lady Valentine said with a haughty head tilt. "I'll find one who is prepared to let me go."

"That's not how the law works," Sergeant Matthers said.

"Sir Gerald deserved to die," Lady Valentine said bitterly.

"I'm sure the police will do everything they can to recover your lost funds, but it's too late for you." Sergeant Matthers stood firm under Lady Valentine's withering glare. "Where is the murder weapon?"

After a few seconds of glowering, Lady Valentine sighed. "I had little time and knew Lady M would wonder where I'd got to. I washed the cane as best I could and hid it in the back of a cupboard full of cleaning supplies."

"Thank you," I said. "And now you must go with Sergeant Matthers."

Lady Valentine gave me a pleading look. "Wouldn't you have done the same thing in my position?"

I considered the recent brawl I'd had with Finella after she'd nearly taken away the creature I loved so dearly. "We often act in ways we don't expect when the things we care most about are at risk."

She gave me a brief nod. "I knew you'd understand."

I didn't. But now wasn't the time for a heated debate.

After accepting a welcome cup of tea from the transport police, I set off on the journey home on the return train.

When I got back to London, I was tempted to join Sergeant Matthers at the police station to witness Inspector Finchley's expression upon realising his previous suspects were innocent.

It was a temptation I resisted, but I'd be sure to check on Dirk. He had quite some story to write now this business was over.

Before going home to scandalise my mother with the outcome of the investigation, I drove to Lady M's house. I was eager to reunite with Benji.

And to ensure his full recovery, and mine, we'd be relaxing for the next few days while I watched over him and enjoyed delicious home-cooked meals.

I climbed out of the car and stretched.

Light feminine laughter reached my ears. Lady M must have company. The laughter came again. It sounded so familiar.

Benji's joyful bark from inside the house suggested whoever was with Lady M was making him happy.

How odd. Lady M occasionally invited me to her summer parties as Ruby's guest, but I couldn't recall Benji growing overly fond of anyone at those events. He liked Lady M well enough, but that wasn't who was laughing.

Rather than announcing myself at the front door, I walked around the side of the building, following the sounds of chatting and laughter.

I stopped by a slightly open window and peered inside. Lady M was settled in front of a pianoforte. Benji lounged on the nearby sofa. There was nobody else in the room, so who had Lady M been talking to?

I only had to wait a few seconds to find out.

Ruby walked into the room, carrying an armful of clothing. "These are beautiful, but I'm not sure they're my style."

"Take it all and donate what you don't want. I have far too many clothes." Lady M moved her fingers lightly over the keys on the pianoforte.

"I can do something with them," Ruby said. "Although it would have been fun to buy a whole new wardrobe."

"Your figure will soon snap back," Lady M said. "And you need to save those pennies for what's coming."

I was still in shock at seeing Ruby in Lady M's house. What were they talking about? How long had Ruby been back? And why hadn't Lady M told me she'd found her?

"Perhaps I shall remain fat and happy forever," Ruby said with a laugh, dropping the pile of dresses onto the back of a chair.

What I saw made my blood freeze and then overheat. When Ruby stood in profile to me, it was clear she was pregnant.

Historical note

Cricket: An English Love Affair

Cricket is usually called a game for gentlemen. The curious sport is fondly held in many hearts and not just in the United Kingdom. But it is here it sticks as a part of our culture, connected to a bygone era of old-fashioned values and jolly good sports.

I grew up a 15-minute walk from a cricket ground and was often astonished by the fierce loyalty people had for cricket. They'd travel for hours to watch a game and endure cold and blazing heat with no shelter.

The fascination with this sport has been going on for some time. The earliest mention of cricket dates back to the 16th century, when a cricket match was recorded at Chevening in Kent between teams representing the Downs and the Weald.

Part of cricket's enduring charm revolves around the notion of fair play, honour, and respect among players. There are curious unwritten rules, such as acknowledging an opponent's achievements or applauding a player for reaching a milestone.

There is also the bonding aspect of cricket, with many matches taking place at a grassroots level, encouraging communities to come together. You'll often find a local village match in your typical 1950s murder mystery (Father Brown, for example.) But cricket reaches the lofty heights of county championships and international tests, uniting countries through the sport.

Part of the nation's love of the sport is its connection to long hot summers, taking tea and eating scones and jam while watching a good old game of cricket. Just writing those words made me feel nostalgic for a time I've never experienced first-hand. It's an escape from the always hectic, never switched off frisson of our modern life.

The Jolly Cricketer Pub: I loosely based the pub in this book on the Lord's Tavern in London. The tavern sits in the centre of London and is a cricket-themed pub connected to Lord's Cricket Club. The club itself began in 1787, and was opened by Thomas Lord on Dorset Fields in Marylebone, but later moved more than once, before settling in 1814 in St John's Wood. Lord's is often referred to as the home of cricket.

Delicious food: Cricket, food, and drink have always been connected, with players stopping for official 20-minute tea breaks (although they don't have to drink tea!) In most mysteries where cricket features, you'll find people picnicking in deckchairs or enjoying an outdoor afternoon tea. How scrumptious! I haven't the foggiest about the rules of cricket but I do know how to enjoy an afternoon tea.

About the author

Immerse yourself into Kitty Kildare's cleverly woven historical British mysteries. Follow the mystery in the Veronica Vale Investigates series and enjoy the dazzle and delights of 1920s England.

Kitty is a not-so-secret pen name of established cozy mystery author K.E.O'Connor, who decided she wanted to time travel rather than cast spells! Enjoy the twists and turns.

Join in the fun and get Kitty's newsletter (and secret wartime files about our sleuthing ladies!)

Newsletter: https://BookHip.com/JJPKDLB
Website: www.kittykildare.com
Facebook: www.facebook.com/kittykildare